■ ABOUT THE AUTHOR ■

Charlotte Edwards is a longtime, multitalented writer originally from Erie, Pennsylvania. At various times in her life a radio announcer, journalist and actress, she is also the published author of four inspirational books, a novel, and 150 articles and short stories, a number of which appear in this volume for the first time since their original publication in popular women's magazines of the '40s and '50s. Much of her writing has been drawn from personal experience, a commodity she possesses in great abundance and loves to share. Her most recent work is a book for new writers entitled *Writing from the Inside Out*, published in March 1984 by Writer's Digest Books.

Despite her prolific and checkered career, Charlotte still found the time to marry and have a son, and she currently lives with her husband in a small town in Maryland.

D0830427

A COLLECTION OF

ROMANTIC NOSTALGIA

SHORT LOVE STORIES
BY CHARLOTTE EDWARDS

Harlequin Books

TORONTO · NEW YORK · LONDON
AMSTERDAM · PARIS · SYDNEY · HAMBURG
STOCKHOLM · ATHENS · TOKYO · MILAN

A COLLECTION OF ROMANTIC NOSTALGIA

The publisher acknowledges Charlotte Edwards as the copyright holder of the following component stories:

Lonesome Saturday
Copyright 1952

Posies for Pamela
Copyright 1948

Love Is Too Young
Copyright © 1956

Man of My Dreams
Copyright 1954

Life Begins on Friday Night
Copyright 1950

Make Up Your Mind, Darling
Copyright 1953

It's Not So Bad to Be a Woman
Copyright 1945

·A COLLECTION OF·
ROMANTIC
NOSTALGIA

LONESOME SATURDAY

For the first eight months in the city Anne-Julie was happy as a cricket. She liked her big old room, partitioned off to enclose a small bath and a tiny kitchenette. She liked the little restaurants hidden in strange places. She liked the Academy of Music, the student recitals at Curtis Institute and the dearest of all havens, the big, beautiful library.

Aunt Elly had approved of books. "You'll never be a lost soul if you have words to lay your eyes on," she used to say. "If you can put yourself into a book, you can live a dozen lives."

Aunt Elly was a rare and special person. Anne-Julie missed her deeply but couldn't begrudge her going, she had been sick so long.

It was fun, those eight months, to get up in the morning and run the exciting gauntlet of traffic through Philadelphia's narrow, jumbled streets, to walk into the immaculate interior of the insurance building, to ride upward in the zooming elevator, settle at her own desk, take dictation from carefully groomed men with morning-scraped cheeks and firmly modulated voices.

But she appreciated, most of all, how nice the girls were to her. "Annie," they called her almost at once. They imposed on her a little. She was the one who went out for coffee, sharpened pencils and did extra typing when her own work was finished. It was quite all right with her. She was allowed to lunch with them, one of a bright, gay group. They let her furnish a soft kind of sounding board for their brittle chatter. They accepted her.

Sometimes it was such a far cry from Aunt Elly's farm in Delaware that she couldn't believe it. The denim trousers and boys' faded shirts had been replaced by the jumpers she loved and the clean, crisp blouses.

Lora, the glamorous one, said to her once, "I must say you know your type, Annie—those little-girl pinafore things, with your big dark eyes and sort of innocent air."

It was high and serious praise.

So it went along nicely, thank you. Except sometimes in the middle of the night she'd wake up listening. After a while she knew it was for the rooster's crow—that old red Benny, who never waited for sunrise but always had to speak his piece in the darkest hours. Then she'd feel strange for a little.

But that was all, until a Saturday morning in October.

Through the window beside Anne-Julie's desk an impudent sun caught on the rims of her typewriter keys and threw little dazzling highlights into her eyes. Under her fingers the reports of the Patten National Mutual Life Insurance Company marched neatly along.

Across the busy street, the trees of Independence Square as she looked down on them were plumes of brilliant color. Two flights down, in the Sanford Building, which was right-angled to hers, the young man was bent over his desk, intentness and interest in the very tilt of his head.

In the office the typewriters slowed, the voices picked up tempo. The feeling of Saturday noon was vibrant, stirring up the blood as the day did.

Lora was talking. "He asked me to go down to the shore this weekend. Seems his family has a big cottage there."

Anne-Julie could see it: the stretches of sand, unsullied by crowds of people, the snapping sharp breeze off the ocean, a big open fire to come back to. And a man who thought Lora was a dream.

The other voices chimed in then. Dinner dancing. A Sunday up in Bucks County. The latest play. Carefully made plans. All including a pretty girl—and a man.

That's when the contentment began to slip. Anne-Julie, her fingers still flying, reviewed her weekend. The new book she'd promised herself. A refurbishing of her wardrobe. A self-administered shampoo and manicure and maybe a standing-room ticket for something musical. Suddenly the small, careful activities sat like lead on her heart.

"David and I," she heard herself saying clearly, "are going to stay in town." Her hand rose quickly to her mouth, astounded at the words.

There was a moment's surprised silence. Then Lora asked, "David? Who's David, Annie?"

Oh, I know what you think of me, Anne-Julie told them silently. *You think I'm no competition. I've learned my little typing course and my shorthand and I'm delighted just to practice them.* Well, it's true enough, her mind acknowledged. But she felt her mouth curling, felt the dimple at one corner tightening. *Why, I don't belong to myself at all,* she thought, knowing her eyes were growing wide and mischievous. It was fun.

"He's my beau," she announced demurely, and let her fingers type out a few phrases.

They clustered around her then.

Lora cried, "Where did you find him?"

Where, indeed? "We met at the concert in January," she found herself saying airily. "Mutual friends."

"What does he look like?" Lora persisted, winking at the girls, and Anne-Julie had a sudden vision of Lora's thoughts. A skinny young man with thick glasses and practically no hair, with nervous hands and a high, uncertain voice.

"He's not terribly tall," she answered dreamily. Her eyes focused out the window. The young man in the Sanford Building leaned back in his chair, tipped his chin high and stretched his powerful arms.

Of course, his name was probably Horatio or Ignatz, she told herself, but he looked like a David. For the past three months she'd thought about him a lot.

Her voice began to take on the ring of truth as she described the dark, curly head, now lit by the sun, the flat, tanned cheeks, the definite chin, the easygoing mouth.

"And his shoulders," she finished triumphantly, "are as broad as a barn, and he wears beautiful old comfortable clothes."

Awe filled the office. That, and an unasked question. "What," the question went, "does such a man ever see in you?"

A little bell broke the tension. Anne-Julie stood up, put the cover on her typewriter and faced her co-workers.

"He's very romantic," she said, laughing, making it sound both embarrassing and endearing. "He calls me his own true love."

They laughed, too. But even Lora looked a little stunned, as if she might have been missing something.

Anne-Julie had shot her bolt. The warmth of its explosion got her down in the elevator and out onto the brilliant street. It was a shame to have it end, the feeling of anticipation, of preciousness, that her amazing words had created. She walked along slowly, watching the flip of her skirt in the windows, noting how neat and small and anonymous she looked and arguing with Aunt Elly, who hated a lie above all things.

"It wasn't a lie, really, Aunt Elly," she explained seriously under her breath. "It's like the games I used to play in the hayloft. When I was a princess, remember? And sometimes a cowgirl. Or a famous actress."

Aunt Elly seemed to accept the explanation. Perhaps she, too, remembered Anne-Julie's fear of Long John, and the time she was Alice and insisted she could walk right through a looking glass.

At the corner Anne-Julie hesitated. There it was, the Sanford Building. On impulse, this day of impulsiveness, she stopped, giggled nervously, then stood quietly at the trolley stop, watching the building entrance.

He came out finally, slowly and quite alone. He pulled a worn pipe from his pocket, filled it calmly from a pouch, scratched a match with a deft fingernail and puckered his nice mouth around the stem until the pipe puffed smoke signals above his head.

Something began to bubble in Anne-Julie. It was light and fluffy and filled with a sort of magic that could not be denied. She gave in to it with barely a struggle.

He turned to the left and sauntered down the street. Anne-Julie sauntered, too. Individually they avoided the busy people. They looked around at the weathered old buildings, at the sooty windows filled with all sorts of things, and suddenly a strange thing happened to Anne-Julie. Her imagination took over and she was up there beside David and his strong hand was on her elbow.

"It's so good to know you at last," he was saying close to her ear to shut out the passersby. "I've been keeping an eye on you for months, you know. There's something so pristine, so elegant, about the way you sit at your typewriter—"

Anne-Julie laughed softly.

"So," he went on, "this is like a dream."

"It is a dream," she put in gently.

"You don't think it's too sudden, do you?" he was asking anxiously. "It came to me like lightning, like a blizzard, like a stroke of pure sun. 'There,' I told myself, looking up as I'll always look up to you, 'is my own true love.'"

Anne-Julie quivered with the beauty of it. Then she bumped into a fat woman, arms full of parcels, voice full of snarls, and awoke abruptly in the middle of the real world.

Ahead of her, David was cutting across the street easily, as if all cars would ignore him and he were wrapped in a sort of personal untouchableness.

Anne-Julie cut across after him. *It pays*, she thought, *to be small and brown and inconspicuous. I'm exactly the kind of person they choose for spies or for lady detectives. Nobody notices me, even if they see me a dozen times.*

The idea came then, and it made the day seem full.

Something to do and somebody to do it with. She didn't allow herself to think that he might be going places she couldn't. She just took one step at a time, more careful of traffic than David but just as sure.

She paced behind him into Independence Square. She sat on the bench next to his. She looked at the trees and the children and glimpsed the Liberty Bell through the old doors opened to the day. But from the tips of her eyes she saw David clearly, the way he crossed his knees, folded his arms against his chest and leaned his head back on the bench, his eyes closed, soaking up the shadow and the sun and the little breeze that was going nowhere at all and was in no hurry to get there.

She said to David, not even moving her mouth but

sure he would understand, "All those people, David. They look tired, they look ready to snap. None of them seems happy."

"Except us, " David was murmuring back to her. "We're peaceful and contented because we're outdoors. Because we're together."

"I knew you'd love room around you," she said.

"I was brought up on a farm. In Maine."

Anne-Julie sat quietly, listening to David's description of Maine, which she had never seen. After a while he reached for her hand and stopped talking. She closed her eyes.

When she opened them, the bench next to hers was empty. She jumped up and glanced around frantically. On the top step of the entrance to the hall she spied the familiar shoulders and for a minute she felt weak with relief. She hurried across the park. She ran up the stairs. She slowed and stood behind David, a little to his left.

The high-lofted room rang with the voices of schoolchildren as it always did, but David seemed alone in a pool of his own quietness. He reached out slowly and stretched one finger along the great speaking crack, as if he had been there, had shared the joy that was too big even for the bright new bell.

"You're wonderful," Anne-Julie whispered to him. "You're just the way I knew you would be."

She stayed far behind him as he walked into the other rooms, as he read the documents slowly, like one of the schoolchildren.

She listened for his imagined voice and it came to her.

"Darling," he said, "you see how it was with them—how bold their signatures were, how proud? Have we forgot too much of it?"

Anne-Julie hadn't thought it out, but she found the answer coming easily. "We just let it get covered up a little," she reassured him. "It's the same. In Maine. In Delaware. Right here."

She found herself nodding, then realized she was patterning her gesture to the slight nod of David's head, there beside the showcases. *We've even come to the same conclusion,* she told herself delightedly.

Her feet felt light and dancing as they went down the front steps and back to the busy street. David stopped at the corner, looked around him, then on impulse moved toward a slowing trolley. Anne-Julie had to run to get inside the closing doors.

She sat down in the first seat, her hands shaking and her heart moving fast. David was behind her now and he'd probably get out the middle door, and how would she know without switching her head every block? No dream talk came to her. Abruptly she was a girl alone on a crowded trolley.

Slowly, slowly she turned her head, chin tipped, apparently studying the ads pasted high above the windows. She managed to see him then, three seats behind her—on the outside, thank goodness.

Everything became all right again. "I am enchanted by your profile," he seemed to whisper.

She shook her head slightly. "I've always been—chagrined about my nose," she whispered back. "Snub."

"Tilted," he corrected.

He rose from the seat and headed for the center exit. Anne-Julie pulled quickly up, let two people get between them and got off after him.

I feel like a bloodhound, she thought. She smiled so gaily that a white-haired gentleman, momentarily blocking her view of David, grinned back.

Why, somebody noticed me, she told herself. *I'll have to be careful.*

David was walking with purpose through the doors of a drugstore. For the first time Anne-Julie realized that, were she beside him, she would reach just about to his shoulder. It pleased her. She stretched herself tall, cut in and around the customers and followed him down the length of the soda fountain.

When David sat down, Anne-Julie chose a stool a discreet five places away from him. Other customers were separating them, but she could study him in the long narrow mirror behind the fountain. His lashes were very long and black. What color were his eyes?

"It's no fun to eat alone, is it?" she asked his distant reflection.

"What'd you say, ma'am?" the white-capped boy on the other side of the counter asked.

Anne-Julie felt a blush rise to her cheeks. *Careful,* she reprimanded herself. *I'm muttering now.* She beamed at the young man. He beamed back. He was the first young man in all of Philadelphia to look at her with admiration.

She ordered a milk shake, and when it was before her, it didn't seem in the least strange that David should have one set in front of him, too.

"Quick energy," she thought of him as saying. "Not that this city milk can compare in any way with our good old cow's milk back in Maine. Do you remember how it was in the barn, Anne-Julie? Warm and fragrant, with that sweet-sour smell of hay and animals. And the kittens in the secluded corners and always a shaggy, happy-tailed dog." He sighed.

She wanted to tell him then. She wanted to say, "Someday, David, I'll have a real surprise for you. I'm landed gentry, believe it or not. Aunt Elly left me the whole farm—all five hundred acres of it. The tenant farmers keep it going for me. But someday we'll go back there."

The sweep of the farm laid itself out before her eyes and homesickness rocked her. She shook her head to wipe away the vision.

She stood boldly behind David while he paid for his shake. She handed the cashier her money and followed him out the door.

The afternoon was half gone, and with it vanished the bright noon sun. In its place was a tentative sort of warmth, overlaid with the promise of fall, the threat of winter. The soft little breeze had gained muscles from somewhere and had a push to it, irritable and shivering.

David pulled up his collar around his throat. Anne-Julie imitated him. He walked more briskly now, and it was a little hard to keep up.

"Where to, darling?" Anne-Julie asked him.

He seemed to bend his head toward her, smiling. His eyes were blue—no, they were gray; or were they amber?

"Just you wait and see," he answered. "Every day should have one small secret. This is yours."

The bookstore was old and dim, long and narrow. David moved slowly past the jumbled table displays.

Anne-Julie clung close to the shelves, as far away from him as possible in the small place. The heat of a little gas stove warmed up the old leather, the slick-paper jackets. Anne-Julie pulled out a book of poetry. She held it open. Every pore of her listened.

Because this time, this small time, she didn't have to pretend to hear him. He was really speaking to the frail, white-haired proprietor.

"I promise you I'll find something," he was saying. "But mostly I just want to look. It's that kind of day, don't you think?"

Oh, but his voice was just right. Softer than she'd imagined it, but just as deep. "Here's *Treasure Island*," he murmured, as if it were a miracle. "How I used to love that book."

"Twenty-five cents only," the proprietor insinuated.

"I bet Long John never scared you." Anne-Julie beamed at David. "I bet you swashbuckled through every bit of it."

"And *The Three Musketeers*," David went on.

He tucked the two volumes under his arm, dug into

his pocket and handed the proprietor a fifty-cent piece. He turned around, swiveled past Anne-Julie's back and went out again into the street.

"Nothing, thank you, nothing," Anne-Julie called to the proprietor's lifted eyebrows, and hurried through the door. It seemed very cold after the stuffiness of the old bookshop.

"I'm having such fun," she cried to David's back. "We're doing exactly what I like to do best."

"Of course," David's voice answered her. "I knew it would be like this." He turned into the revolving doors of a large department store.

It was harder to follow him here among the shoppers, but Anne-Julie managed it. Her heart was a feather within her. She felt as she had in the years of her childhood—as if something wonderful were just about to happen, would come true in an hour, in twenty minutes, in two seconds.

David stopped at the jewelry counter. He put his books down and lifted a pair of earrings, a charm bracelet.

Anne-Julie stood frozen at the handkerchief counter, shook her head numbly at the inquiring clerk and watched her hands shake. All the day's joy went drizzling into nothing, so slowly that at first she didn't realize what was happening, or why.

But she understood it at last, watching David hand the charm bracelet to the pretty girl behind the counter, watching him count out money and wait for change, his face happy and relaxed, a pucker to his lips that denoted an under-the-breath whistle.

Of course he'd have a girl to buy things for. Or even a wife. Of course he'd go home now, to some suburb, and have dinner. He'd read the paper, listen to the radio or go to a movie. With that girl. With his wife.

She made up his conversation again. This time it wasn't directed to her. It was aimed at a vague figure, undoubtedly slick and beautiful.

"I knew you wouldn't be home this afternoon, darling, so I just wandered around town. Waiting for you. Always waiting for you."

You wandered, Anne-Julie thought mournfully as the clerk handed David a giftwrapped box, *followed by a sad brown ghost. A wistful, foolish little ghost who had a lovely time with a set of paints that changed the tint of everything around her. Only they were watercolors, you see, David. They washed right off. Right off.*

The tears in her eyes blurred the lights of the store to foggy stars, melted David's figure—his retreating figure now—into something without substance. Out of habit Anne-Julie started to follow him, and was snared by a little voice.

"Annie," it called. "Wait a minute."

She turned, rubbing quickly at her cheeks, to face Lora.

"Are you in a hurry?" Lora cried, coming up to her in that rush that was so exciting, her words spraying like perfume all around her. "I want you to see my new pink feathered hat. Isn't it a love?"

Anne-Julie cast one last glance toward David, whirled by the doors into the afternoon that was almost twilight. *Let him go,* she thought wistfully. *It was a wonderful date, a beautiful time, but he has to go back where he belongs.*

"I'm in no hurry," she managed to Lora. "And your hat is very special."

Lora linked an arm through hers and led her past the silverware, the linens, the bath towels, the men's shirts, shorts and ties, out of the store.

"I thought you had great plans for today," Lora cried gaily. "What was all that about doing the town with your beau?"

Pride took over. Anne-Julie found her voice, once more gay, cheerful and lying. "We've done part of it," she said. "I'm meeting him for dinner. Just on my way home to clean up." She smiled and sighed. "A long bubble bath will be just the thing. David is so—energetic."

It sounded all right, even to her, and apparently to Lora.

"We're leaving in half an hour, too," Lora said, cozy with Anne-Julie for the first time, making her one of the popular girls for whom men were waiting. "Dickie had to work late and I'm to meet him at the station." She smiled lovingly at her reflection. "Have fun," she cried, and signaled a taxi.

Anne-Julie stood on the curb, her waving hand, slowly growing limp. It was dark. The streetlights popped out like lit balloons. She was tired. More tired than her feet or her legs or the dull ache in her temples. Tired inside, where she had always been rested before. At last she turned, feeling strangely confused, now that David was no longer there to lead the way.

But he was! Three doors down, in sight of the department store entrance, the familiar shoulders were silhouetted by the cheerful lights of a restaurant that threw out the crimson information that it was Barney's Lobster Bar.

Instinctively then Anne-Julie's feet swirled her in an about-face. Toward her apartment, away from the restaurant and David and all the nonsense of the afternoon. Just because he was gazing at ruby-red lobsters sleeping on a bed of silver ice didn't mean that his wife was nonexistent, for pity's sake. And chasing a man around town in the bright sunshine, with thousands of people close, was one thing. Following him after dark, down streets thinned of humanity, was decidedly another.

So spoke her good sensible mind. So spoke Aunt Elly.

But it doesn't take long to form a habit. Wanting to see what David was going to do next proved stronger than common sense. At the very moment when her turned-around feet were waiting for a decisive command, her pretending put words in her ears again.

"I always feel a little sorry for them," she heard herself murmur, feeling David's sleeve against her own, seeing the lobsters as clearly as if her nose were pressed against the window. "It seems like such a horrible fate to be boiled alive."

"My tender little girl." David laughed at her. "Let's go in and have a couple of them murdered, shall we?"

At his imagined question, Anne-Julie found herself once more facing the still form, once more moving toward it, keeping in the shadow of the buildings, walking very slowly so that he might have a chance to precede her.

But he didn't move. The space between them narrowed with a frightening sort of inevitability and Anne-Julie's heart began to bump against her ribs.

What will I do, she thought. *I'll just have to swing out around him and hurry away. Oh, Aunt Elly, I'm such a* dummkopf, *just like you used to call the hired man.*

She tipped her chin high and pulled her shoulders back. There were only two paces between them. She began to figure the angle of swerve when suddenly David switched his head and looked straight at her, intently and sharply.

Panic choked her breath. She turned abruptly and darted through the wide restaurant door.

The place was very bright and crowded. A burly man in a butcher's apron wagged an imperious finger in her direction. She scuttled toward him, reassured by his bulk, trying not to feel the eyes fastened on her from outside. Blue, she knew they were now.

"There's one table left, lucky you," the man said. She followed him, expert now in the process, to a small table at the very back of the room, next to the

uge barbecue. She slid as far down as she could in
er seat and held the huge menu before her face.

He wasn't David, that was the whole of it. He was a
tranger. Just as he might have a wife, so might he be a
volf, or a friend of a policeman, or just anybody. One
hing was certain: he'd noticed her. He had waited
here, watching her come out, watching her say good-
ye to Lora, waiting for her to be alone on the dark
treet. Nobody stared at lobsters as long as all that.

And as Aunt Elly always said, terrible things can
appen to girls alone in a big city—if they ask for
rouble.

She swallowed hard. *I certainly asked for it,* she
hought. The prices on the menu came momentarily
o the fore, shocked her briefly and receded again. He
new. He knew she'd been following him all after-
oon, probably. He could draw any kind of conclu-
ion from it. Even if he were perfectly nice, she
ouldn't bear the thought that he should know she'd
een chasing him.

The burly man's voice made her jump.

"Lobster," she half-whispered, glad for the secret
ocket in her purse where she kept rainy-day money.

Please make him go away, she begged. *Aunt Elly,
rake him go away.*

She recoiled as the waiter dangled a live lobster
nder her nose.

"What do I do with that?" she asked through dry
ps.

He grinned. "You approve of it, if you do."

She nodded.

"Okay. Clam chowder in a minute."

With true femininity, Anne-Julie reassured herself
y reaching into her purse, dabbing at her nose with a
owder puff, repairing the line of her lips. It quieted
er hands. Staring into the tiny mirror at her fright-
ned eyes, she shook her head a little, and some of the
anic went away.

*I never heard of a man having a girl arrested fo
following him,* she consoled her image. *Besides, ther
are a hundred people here. I'm perfectly safe. He's boun
to go away.*

She snapped the case shut, put it in her purse an
looked up. The panic returned stronger than ever
Moving slowly and steadily between the tables, heade
toward her with a terrifying determination, was David

When he reached her, he looked down for a mea
sureless moment. Then he asked, "Is this plac
taken?" He sat down, not waiting for an answer.

The waiter put a cup of clam chowder before Anne
Julie, took David's order for lobster and disappeare
before she could gather her forces, before she coul
say, "I've changed my mind. I have to go."

David calmly lined up the worn silver. Even wit
her eyes fastened on the shaking progress of her sou
spoon, Anne-Julie could see his fingers, precise an
careful and really artistic. Which didn't mean a thing
Lots of villains had nice hands.

He spoke at last. He said, "I was waiting for you
Waiting for your friend to leave."

It was going to be worse than she'd dreamed. Sh
hadn't pictured his closing in like this. But she wasn
Aunt Elly's niece for nothing. She stiffened. She pu
down the spoon.

"I beg your pardon?" she asked in a voice that cam
out just right, cool and formal. She allowed her lids t
rise and willed haughtiness into her eyes.

He looked away, out over the room. He said, "I'v
never believed in coincidence...."

Oh, dear, Anne-Julie thought. Oh, dear, oh, dea
oh, dear.

She braced herself. She opened her mouth. *Maybe
I make a clean breast of it,* she thought frantically
Maybe if I just apologize and then get up and out of her

But he didn't look at her. He continued to scan the room and his voice went on. "Until today, that is," he added, "I saw you first in the square, I—I liked the way you looked. So—clean—" A hard red flush climbed slowly up his cheeks.

Something in Anne-Julie loosened a little. She knew all about blushes.

"That would have been all." He picked up speed. You just don't go up to strange girls in the park and say, 'I'd like to know you.' No matter how lonely you are. But—all afternoon—"

Anne-Julie felt her own cheeks begin to match his.

"In the hall, the trolley, the drugstore. I tried to get up nerve enough to speak to you in the bookshop. I went into the department store because—well. I couldn't look over my shoulder and I was afraid I'd lost you. But even there—" He pulled out the charm bracelet. He smiled a little, still not looking at her. "I even got hooked into buying this."

Anne-Julie swallowed, easily this time, and her face felt deliciously cool.

"It seemed too strange—such a miracle—that you were doing the same things I like to do." He moved his head toward her. He looked straight at her. His eyes were blue, all right, honest and shy. "I waited outside Barney's. It's my favorite eating place. I told myself, 'If she likes lobster, if she comes in here—I'll speak to her.'" He shrugged and moved his hands outward. "It just seemed to me as if we were—meant to know each other. Coincidence. Fate." His eyes this time, when they met hers, held, and like the blush it was something Anne-Julie understood. My goodness, he wasn't the only lonesome person in Philadelphia.

"Just imagine," she said demurely, "both of us being in all those places at exactly the same time. And never even noticed." She smiled widely to cover the whopper. "It's enough to make anybody believe in fate."

Someday, she thought smugly, *maybe I'll tell hi*
that sometimes Fate needs a nudge and I nudged he
Only it would be a shame to spoil a faith like tha
Maybe, though, some other Saturday, just like toda
only real.

David relaxed. He looked happy. "Maybe I'd bette
introduce myself."

See, Aunt Elly, Anne-Julie chortled defiantly.
didn't tell a lie, after all. I've got a beau. Horatio d
Ignatz or David—I've got a beau!

POSIES
FOR
PAMELA

All right, so maybe my shoulders aren't constructed like the span of the Memorial Bridge. There are other things in life. The fact that a man stands six-four, with snake-dancing muscles, doesn't prove much. In some fields, that is. As my war record will testify, much as my modesty deplores quoting past performances.

Of course, the minute a boy begins to attain man's estate and discovers that he's not going to have Atlas' stature, he prepares himself for self-defense. Not in a vulgar fashion, always. Not with his fists. But he learns to have a quick tongue. He learns to stay away from the dangerous situation. And learns to pour on charm with the ladies.

It leads straight to the ladies, of course. What doesn't?

My mother was a very quick and busy woman, and quite a beauty, too. Somehow, loyalty to her own sex was left right out of her nature. Which was a good thing. Not only did my father worship her till the day she died, but she gave me some tips that have been very useful to me in my business.

"Women can't help it, Larry," she'd say. "When a great dark giant comes walking toward them with the Stone Age look in his eyes, they just wilt. But let them hook the giant for keeps and they fret all over the place. First off, they know other women wilt when he's around. Which does not make for peace of mind. Then, after a while, almost all women like to have a man they can talk to."

I learned to talk to women.

My mother also made the statement, "It may be trite to say that women love little courtesies and attentions and good manners. But like a great many trite things, it's also terribly true. Many a woman has stood by a scoundrel simply because he managed to make her feel like a queen."

I learned to make women feel special and precious.

My mother knew whereof she spoke. Even if she did draw her deductions as vicarious praise of my father, a small neat man with beautiful manners and a real deference to womanhood.

It worked. It started working in high school. Girls who practically clawed one another to streamers for the privilege of being escorted to dances by the football players would spend the greatest part of the evening in my arms. I learned a few tricky steps that football players' big feet couldn't seem to navigate. I also learned a few tricky phrases that, whispered into a shell-pink ear, had nothing to do with signals or training or muscles.

All of which in turn has little or nothing to do with Pamela Crane and the love that opened like a water lily in my heart when she first walked into my shop.

I had the shop before I went away. I came back to it and civilization, filled with a zest that ignored rehabilitation. The minute I opened the door and smelled the sweet flood reaching out to me, I was at home. Maxie—she was my helper before the war, and she kept things going in fine shape while I was away—

said that I turned white around the gills with pure sensuous pleasure, and maybe she was right.

Did I mention I own and operate just about the rosiest little flower business in Anchor City? No puns intended.

Anyhow, the first time I saw Pamela it was winter outside, spring inside, and peaceful as all get-out. That is, until that moment when I stepped out of the back room where we do the fancy finger stuff, bows and blending and snipping, and looked up at her.

I am sorry to have to report that I looked up. It always seems a great disadvantage. Not to me, of course. But to the general public. Ludicrous. Mr. and Mrs. Henpeck. Be not fooled. Napoleon was no slouch, off as well as on the battlefield. But there I am, on the defensive again.

Anyway, the quiet peace went out of me like a snuffed candle. In its place came a blaze that I can only liken to a prairie fire on the rampage. For a moment, the heat and intensity and sweep of it smothered me. So that all I could do was try to breathe. And stare at her.

She was something to stare at. She wore a bright red fuzzy coat. Her head was bare. Fat and slowly melting flakes of snow starred its blondness. In an age when girls swung their hair about their shoulders, Pamela brushed hers to a golden shine and knotted it thickly and neatly in the back.

I was waiting for her voice to knock me out. When it came, it very nearly did. Soft, low, womanly, almost shy. Ah!

"I'd like to order some funeral flowers," she said.

The words wafted around my head. "Funeral flowers," I beamed. Then I drew my mouth serious and let the horror get into my eyes. "No one close to you, I hope," I moaned.

"Quite close," she answered calmly.

"I'm so sorry," I murmured. An undertaker

couldn't have said it with more unction. Only he wouldn't have been as sincere as I was.

She really looked at me. "You don't have to go to pieces," she remarked. "It's my Uncle Horace. He turned eighty-six last November seventeenth. He had a right to die."

"Of course he did. Of course," I said hurriedly. "We all have a right to die sometime."

A little puzzle carved itself between her sleek dark brows.

I decided to change the subject. "Lilies are the usual thing," I said. "Or perhaps you'd like a floral piece. Carnations are popular. But for an uncle of yours..." I paused. I was once more lost and smothered.

"For an uncle of mine..." she prompted.

I gasped and went on, inspired. "It must be something different, rare, expressive. It must be brilliant purples and a touch of white—with gray and green interwoven..." I could see it. Small flowers, old-fashioned, suitable for eighty-six hard-lived years.

Pamela frowned again. "I don't know," she said. "I never did this sort of thing before. But mother has the flu. It can't cost more than six dollars. Can we get anything decent for six dollars?"

You can get my shop, my heart screamed. *You can have every blasted orchid in it, yes, and the gardenias, too, and that precious little plant that Maxie and I have been nursing along for the past eighteen months. You can have me and my two-year-old car, and my three good suits, and the recordings of the* Messiah *and Fats Waller. And you can keep the six bucks, beautiful.*

My lips had more sense. "Oh, yes," I assured her. I sounded quiet and unlike a psycho for the first time since I'd seen her. "I'll see that you get something very nice."

I watched her hands count out the six one-dollar bills, glad that they were singles so that I could watch longer. It would have been nice if those red-tipped fingers counted out the dimes of a piggy bank. That would have taken quite a time. Quite a time.

I watched her pivot and move toward the door. I saw the white snow waiting to make its background for her. I noticed, not very casually, that her legs tapered from a slim roundness down to a slimmer neatness. With her hand on the knob she swung abruptly to face me. I pulled my eyes quickly upward. The prairie fire engulfed my cheeks.

"You'll want to know where to send it," she remarked.

"Where to send it," I repeatedly dully. "Oh, yes. Yes, of course. Your Uncle Horace."

Her lips twitched. "Well, not my Uncle Horace, exactly," she said. "But just see they get to Henders' Funeral Home by tomorrow afternoon."

I pulled a pad toward me. I wrote the words down, the day. Then another thought hit me. "Your name?" I asked importunately. "What is your name?"

She looked surprised. "If it's not a charge..." she began. Then she shrugged, apparently outwitted with the futility of me. "Pamela Crane," she revealed. "One-nineteen Lantern Street."

I didn't need to write that down. It pushed like a sharp pencil with soft lead, firmly into my mind. I was so relieved I almost missed the way she pulled the door gracefully open, shut it quietly, stood for an instant in the doorway, then stepped briskly out, as only long-legged girls can, into the storm.

I stood very still, the worn bills in my hand. After a while Maxie popped into the room.

"What's the matter with you, Squirt?" she asked. "You look all goose flesh. Been in a draft?"

Considering that Maxie is one of the few girls who underinch me to the measurement of three, that "Squirt" has never irritated me. Until that moment, I mean.

"There is nothing the matter with me," I replied with dignity. "And please don't call me Squirt."

Maxie smiled, that lopsided business that always seems to take the world in with her on a good joke. "Okay, Squirt," she agreed.

"Your hair's a mess," I said. "And why have I never seen Pamela Crane before?"

Maybe it was her instinctive gesture to her rumpled black hair that emptied her face of its grin. Because it was back again in a moment as pert as her words.

"Aha, so that's it." She ticked off on her fingers. "One, Pam came to Anchor City when you were in the Battle of the Bulge. Two, you haven't seen her around because you've buried yourself under floral constructions ever since you got back. Three, she lives alone with her mother and her just-deceased Uncle Horace. Four, she's a tearing beauty who has all the boys on edge. And five, she's too tall for you."

I digested four and ignored five. I wondered. "How do you happen to know so much about her?"

Maxie smiled. This time I didn't like it. "Because for almost a year now Joe has done nothing but sigh and pant for her. It's like living with an asthmatic bear."

My heart took an elevator plunge. Joe was Maxie's brother. Joe was two years younger than I am and a good eight inches taller. Joe was as dark and curly headed as Maxie and much more serious about the eyes. Joe was the heart's delight of half the feminine population of Anchor City. And had been from the day before he put on long pants.

I went into the back room and robbed the till for little purple flowers and fine green ferns and soft white rosebuds. My fingers worked the way I like them to. But my mind was busy with a campaign.

I'd done it before. I could do it again, now, this time, when it really counted. I pulled out every word of wisdom my mother had given me and stacked it against Joe's magnificent physique, his slow happy smile, the way he bent his head down, down toward the ladies.

Maxie came out. "Migosh," she yelped. "There's $22.98 worth of tribute in that masterpiece if there's one thin dime."

"So what?" I countered, looping and doubling intensely.

"So I put the six dollars in the cash register," she said quietly. And walked out.

After Maxie left that night I stayed behind. I didn't want her around for what I was going to do. It took me till midnight. But it was worth it.

The snow had stopped and a white hush was over the world. I drove slowly, down Main, over Atherton, and turned right into Lantern. One-nineteen was an old brown house, looking for all the world like a fat rusty hen squatting in a nest of cotton. The windows were all dark.

I passed the house, pulled up to the curb and turned the engine off. I got out like a thief in the night. The snow helped to muffle my tiptoed steps. The porch was a mile wide. I open the storm door, holding my breath, and put the little package, newspaper wrapped against its cellophane, in what looked like the warmest corner. Then I went home and slept as if I'd been thirty-six hours in combat. I didn't even dream. The campaign had begun.

The package? A tiny nosegay, no bigger than a bracelet, of the smallest, most exquisite flowers I could manage. The card said, "If you lived in the age of your beauty, this nosegay would declare itself yours." I didn't sign it.

The first thing I thought of in the morning was *Uncle Horace gets himself buried today*. I looked anxiously out the window. It was a good day for it. Suddenly mild and very clear. His soul would have a straight, open space with no heavy clouds from here to heaven.

I put on my most somber suit, a dark tie and a solemn expression. I was very fond of Uncle Horace. He was close to Pamela. Maybe he'd even helped to bring her up. I was grateful to him for the job he'd done.

Maxie looked me over sharply. It's a way she has. I noticed it particularly.

"You look better today," she said at last. "More like you were pulling yourself to yourself, if you know what I mean. Yesterday everything about you was flying like parts of an explosion."

That's Maxie. Crazy. But you get what she means. I pretended not to.

"A man who has been forty-two months in service deserves some moments when he is not entirely integrated," I replied with great dignity.

"Holy potatoes," Maxie answered inelegantly. "You've been out of service since two weeks after V-J Day—which wasn't yesterday, brother."

"No. Not yesterday," I murmured. I slid off into yesterday, seeing the door open again, the sleekness of her hair—

"Joe and I are going to pop corn tonight," Maxie said, interrupting my thoughts. "How's about bringing your records? Cozy evening. Open fire. No talk. Maybe doughnuts?"

I guess the silence must have run pretty thin, because she pinched my ear suddenly. It hurt. I did a double take on her words. "No, thank you," I said at last.

Maxie's red mouth slipped a notch. It was exactly the sort of evening she knew I liked best. But my mind was busy with a camellia, a blush-pink one, set in a ruching of stiff lace. I was already figuring the words to go with it. I managed to see Maxie's eyes pretty clearly, though.

"I—I have made other plans for the evening, Maxie," I said. "Some other time, huh?"

"Some other time," she agreed. Then added, surprisingly, "And I hope you won't regret it."

The camellia came out very well. Even my mother would have admitted that the card was courtly: "The glorious flush of your cheeks, cooled by the snow, warmed by your loveliness—that is this flower."

I locked up the store shortly after ten. There were lights downstairs in Pam's house. I drove on by.

Presently I found myself in front of Maxie's house. There was only one dim lamp, and the uneven warmth of firelight touched against the windows. Impulsively I stopped. I was always welcome at Maxie's, and I had a couple of hours to kill.

Before I put my finger on the buzzer I could hear the closing foolishness of a Hoosier Hot Shot number. Maxie came to the door just as the record hooted to a stop.

"Well now, well now," she jeered. "Minds changed every hour on the hour, greased, lubricated, good as new."

She looked very well for a brunette. For a little girl. She'd brushed her hair for once and her dress was sort of like the firelight. Subdued heat in a quietly crimson way.

I told her so. Habit of years.

Her cheeks seemed rosier with the compliment. Or maybe it was that she was leading me into the lamplight and it lit her up.

I blinked a little in the dimness. Then I made out two pairs of shoulders bending over the records. One was tall and very broad and masculine. Joe, of course. The other—oh, my beating heart—the other was Pamela. Even before they swung around, even before I saw anything but their backs, I thought what a swell-looking pair they were. A fatal thought for a hopeful suitor.

"You know Pamela," Maxie introduced. "At least in a business way. She always gives you her funerals."

Pamela looked a little hurt.

Joe frowned. "That's no way to talk, Maxie," he reproved. "After Pamela just buried her Uncle Horace this very afternoon." Joe, I might say, is a gentle soul. Very different from his sister.

"Quite a job," Maxie said. Then she looked abashed. For her. "I'm sorry, Pam. My rivulet tongue, you know."

Pamela nodded gravely. She took two steps forward and stood looking at me. "The flowers were very beautiful," she said.

For one wild moment I thought she was on to me already, remembering my guilty nosegay. That would have spoiled everything.

"The loveliest ones of all," she went on in that way of hers. "Mother was terribly pleased."

"I'm glad you liked them," I said. "You made me see Uncle Horace so clearly. It was almost as if I'd known him. A shrunken little man, with snow-white hair and wisdom for every occasion."

Maxie and Joe hooted in unison. Pam smiled. I swallowed.

"Round as a barrel," Joe explained. "Bald as a coot. Voice like a foghorn."

I grinned with them. Then I went over to the records and looked for Maxie's Harold Bauer numbers. I was so conscious of Pamela standing by the fire that prickles ran up the back of my fresh haircut.

Before I could spike the records Joe came over and slapped on "Night and Day." I turned around. I had to watch it. I had to see the way he walked slowly toward Pamela, his great long arms reaching out, and how she slid into them. They were something blown by the wind or the music. I didn't like the way it made me feel. Joe didn't have football player's feet. He could dance and so could she.

Maxie went out into the kitchen. I decided it was better not to torture myself. I went along, too.

I leaned against the sink, watching her make coffee as I had half a hundred times before. "So that's what you meant by hoping I wouldn't regret not coming," I said at last.

Her head was bent over the plastic tablespoon. Her mouth moved as she counted. Her hair swooped down against her cheek and hid her expression. "More or less," she said. "More or less."

But I couldn't stay put. In a minute I wandered back into the living room. The record stopped. I put on the Harold Bauer. I sat down on the floor with my back propped against a chair. I watched the firelight reach out to glow Pamela, also on the floor, her long legs tucked neatly, her eyes dark and mysterious.

Maxie called, "Come get this tray, will you, Joe?"

It should have been me. I always helped Maxie at shindigs. But I was glad it wasn't.

When we were alone I said, "Pamela, tell me about yourself. All the things I ought to know."

She turned, a little surprised. "You ought to know? What do you mean?"

I laughed; I heard it, so I guess it sounded easy. I kept my voice low and personal. "Were you a shy, sweet child? Do you like to walk in the rain? What do you think of Charles Boyer? And why haven't I seen you before?"

She smiled. "You're a very unusual person, Larry. Joe said you were. Maxie said you were. They've done a great deal of talking about you. Now I know they were right."

I didn't want to talk about myself. "Everybody's unusual, one way or another," I said. "Take Joe, now—"

Maybe it was my imagination, but I thought her face softened. "Joe," she echoed. I shivered.

Then they were back. The coffee was hot and fragrant, as Maxie's coffee always was. Pretty soon it was after midnight and Pamela was being tucked into the red fuzzy coat by Joe and the door was opening and Maxie was talking a mile a minute.

"Ah," she sighed deeply. "Blondes. Squired by two men, while the dark woman is left to watch the dying embers. Larry, you'd better stay and have a last cup of coffee. Joe will see Pam home."

"Thanks, no, Maxie," I said as lightly as I could. Maxie and I had finished off so much coffee and so many fires. "But I have the car. I'll run Pamela over." I looked up at Joe. "Save your strength, fellow," I insisted. "No use your going out in this cold, too."

Joe looked at Pam. She looked back. For a minute I felt like the ham between two slices of bread, or a splinter in a finger. She nodded.

"Don't bother, Joe," she said. "Larry will be going right past my house."

Joe closed the closet door. He looked grumpy. Like a bear, as Maxie had suggested. "Okay, okay," he mumbled.

Pamela put her hand on his sleeve. "And thank you, Joe," she said softly. "Thank you very much."

"For what?" Joe asked. But you could see him thaw.

I drove slowly, but you can make three blocks last just so long. Pamela didn't say much. She seemed dreamy. So I let the understanding silence pile up until we were before her door.

"I'll see you again, Pamela?" I asked. "Soon? To-morrow? Saturday? Maybe Sunday, too?"

I'd surprised her again. I loved the way the dreamy look snapped away and she became clearly conscious of me. "All or one?" she asked, laughing a little.

"All if possible. One at least."

She pushed a mittened hand against her hair. "But more than one, of course," she said quietly.

The snow melted for me right that moment, as she slipped through the door and left her promise behind. I rode around in the night grown suddenly spring, until the fourth time around the block I saw her light go out. Then I picked up the camellia tenderly, as if it were her hand, and put it in the same corner of the storm door.

I lay awake a long time. I wished with an old and quiet desperation that she hadn't had to look down at me when she'd said good-night.

The rest of the winter went by like snow against the windows. We had a lot of fun. Dancing at different places around town. Evenings at Maxie's. Movies and even one concert. Despite my best efforts, it was always the four of us. Also, somehow Joe and Pamela seemed to stride ahead of Maxie and me. But I bided my time.

I knew a thing or two. I knew that those hours spent in the back room making Pamela's bouquets as varied, as amusing, as romantic as I could would pay dividends. I knew that the words written on those small secret cards would speak well for me when I revealed myself.

In the meantime, I waited and watched her with my posies on her shoulder, in her hair, at her wrist. It was as if I'd set a seal on her, a fragrant stamp, that proclaimed her mine.

She was very curious about the flowers, and delighted. I learned that in practically no time at all.

"It makes me feel so...so like somebody in a book," she said the night Maxie asked her, with a touch of malice in her voice and a leer at me, where they came from. "Every morning when I wake up," Pamela explained in her soft voice, "I rush downstairs to see if there's another one. Mother brings them in and puts them beside my plate."

I could see her, golden hair loosened and flying, something rosy and satin trilling behind her, her slim feet in feathered slippers. I avoided seeing her at the table, reading my careful notes to her mother. I'd met her mother. Fat and white like mashed potatoes, somehow. But maybe Pamela hid the notes.

Maxie's voice was creamy. "It's like something from another age. You know, Knighthood in Flower—and lace on the cuffs." She murmured reflectively, "Nobody ever sends me flowers. Whoever is he, do you suppose?"

I knew the needles were for me. I never felt their nicking. Because Pamela was looking up, the lovely lines of her face drawn taut, her eyes wise and sweet.

"I think I know," she murmured softly. "I think I know."

She was looking up, I said. Which meant she was focusing all that tenderness on friend Joe. Well, he had the grace to look red and foolish, although he didn't deny it. Maxie's eyes, when she looked at me, had the grace to go a little ashamed.

So I knew I had to get hot. No use letting all the gratitude take root in the wrong place. I set a time in my mind.

That plant now, the one Maxie and I had nourished and yearned over for eighteen months. We called it Oscar, because its real name was as long as antidisestablishmentarianism. Anyhow, it was in bud, one perfect deep-red aromatic bud that promised to open within a week.

Friday, I figured it. Friday, February 14, which was also Valentine's Day. Which was also the Valentine Dance at the club. A perfect setup.

I started building up to it. Tuesday's gardenias said, "The time grows shorter, Loveliness. On the day of St. Valentine I shall reveal myself to you."

Wednesday I wrote merely, "To worship at a distance is not enough."

Thursday night I dropped off a dash of mignonette and white violets. "Tomorrow" was all the card said.

I went home and counted all the things I knew about Pamela. It took quite a while. She was beautiful. She liked me. I puzzled her. She was beautiful. We danced very well indeed together. She was beautiful. She liked to talk to me. Occasionally she even made an opportunity, a peaceful little island for two, which shut out Maxie and Joe, when she listened quietly, her perfect chin in her lovely hand. She was beautiful. And she was romantic. She was waiting impatiently for the flowers, the messages, the lover.

I smiled, thinking of Joe. He'd stopped even the little talking he used to do. For the past month Joe had sat, glumness a mask on his face, wherever we were. Those flowers had him plenty worried. They made him clumsy, and guilty, and unsure of himself.

Friday morning I rushed to the shop. I look Oscar carefully from the hand-built corner where we kept him. Sure enough, there he was. More perfect than even Maxie and I had dreamed.

I got out the silver satin ribbon, the heavy tinfoil, the corsage pins, the silver-fluted paper. I sorted the greens and picked out the laciest ones. When everything was neatly around me, I picked up the small shears and poised them for a breathless moment over the newly opened bud.

I began to dive down carefully, just the right length, just the right slant, when, like a breath on my neck, I became conscious of someone behind me. I whirled, as guilty as a boy caught with a hand in the cookie jar. Maxie stood in the doorway, her hands on her small hips. Her eyes blazed fire. Her nostrils flared.

"What," she said, quietly for her, "in the name of places good and bad, do you think you're doing?"

My grin didn't fit my face. Too big and too loose. "I'm cutting Oscar."

She was beside me in a flash. Her hand whipped the shears from mine. "Oh, no you're not," she said. This time she wasn't quiet. "Oh, no you're not." She threw the shears with all her strength clear across the room. I knew a moment's amazement when they landed, as in mumblety-peg, on their points, and shivered back and forth in the dim light.

"Now listen," I began.

"You listen," she cried. "I've watched you rob yourself—rob us—of every decent flower in the place for weeks. I've sat evening after evening while you drooled like a teething baby, or gaped like a hooked fish, at that blond string of macaroni. I've watched your sense of humor deflate into bubble gum. I've even seen some of the mush you've put on those despicable cards." She paused for breath, then went on. "Do you know what she does with those cards? She puts them around her bedroom mirror. Like... like snapshots or dance programs."

That rocked me. I could see Pamela's friends, going up to powder their little noses or comb their little heads, bending to read my carefully printed words.

"What of it?" I managed to ask.

"What of it?" Maxie was really rolling now. "What of it? If that doesn't show you, what will? If that doesn't prove—" Suddenly everything broke. Her eyes. Her tense mouth. Her little tight fists. The tears started to pour down, pushing on one another till they had no separateness. "Go ahead," she said at last, very softly. "Go ahead. Cut Oscar. He's yours, of course. I'm sorry. And I'm quitting."

Before I could move, she was out of the back room. Her heels made a machine-gun sound across the shop. Then the front door opened and closed. I raced after her when I got my bearings. But I couldn't see her anywhere. I went slowly back into the store.

I stood for a long time looking at Oscar. Then I put him back in his warm corner. After all, Maxie had taken the bulb I brought back from the florists' convention, the bulb that had very few mates in the country, the bulb they said would never grow in our climate. She'd planted it and talked to it and put a lot more than fertilizer into it. In a way it was Maxie's flower, too. I really didn't have any right.

I started to assemble what I could find. My stomach

felt the way it does when I eat too much hot apple pie. I told myself that I was disappointed, that's all. Oscar was my climax. It depressed me to give him up.

I also remembered that mirror with my cards around it. And I had never seen Maxie cry before. Not when I went away. Not even when I came back. She must be very fond of Oscar.

When I finished the corsage it was all right. It was very good, really. Tiny sweetheart roses, shading from white to pale pink to bright crimson, shaped like a heart, ruffled like a valentine and backed with a gay red satin bow.

Just before noon Joe called. His voice was gruff and embarrassed. "I want to send Pam some flowers," he said.

"Any special kind?" I kept my tone very business-like.

"Yeah." The pause was so long I knew he was thinking of the flowers Pam had been getting. "Something that suits her."

I tried not to laugh. Joe, getting ideas.

"Sweet peas," he said suddenly. "That's it. A nice big corsage of sweet peas. The pink ones."

"Sweet peas," I said solemnly. *You goon*, I thought. Insipid flower if ever there was one. Even smelled insipid. *So that's what you think suits Pam.* "What do you want on the card?"

He hesitated again. "No card," he said at last.

"No card," I echoed.

"You fix them up, eh?" he asked.

"Sure," I said. "Sure. Say, Joe, you seen Maxie today?"

He sounded puzzled. "Maxie? No. I'm at work. Why? Is she sick?"

"No," I said hurriedly. "She...she just left early. Shopping or something. I just wondered. I'll pick you up about nine." I put the receiver back before he could object.

I fixed the sweet peas up nice and pretty. Joe's box and mine both went out in the afternoon delivery.

I was at Pam's house at eight-thirty. Her mother opened the door and gave me the slab of her hand to touch for a moment. I'd have to learn to like Pam's mother.

In a little while Pamela came down the stairs. The white jersey rippled around her gold slippers. She wore a hooded cape, so I didn't get to see my flowers. She was beautiful.

I said, on impulse, "Something in my eye. Mind if I go upstairs and wash it out?" I raced upward before they could speak.

I set the water running in the washbowl. Then I peeked in the three bedrooms until I located Pam's—pale blue and white and very virginal. I switched on the light. Sure enough, my cards were all around the mirror. They looked like a lot, on display that way.

But when Pam's arm was in mine, when she was beside me in the little world of the car, I forgot them. I said, fast and low, "You are beautiful. You're one of a kind. You're the dream valentine come to life."

She looked at me, pleased. "Larry," she said, "you certainly have a way with you. You say the nicest things. Different things—"

When I had to stop the car in the middle of her sentence, I silently reviewed some of my Army vocabulary. I didn't even get out. I pushed the horn. Let Joe come out himself. As for Maxie, I couldn't believe she would ride with us, furious as she was. But out she came. In black, too, and looking a little taller than usual. Which might have been the way she held her chin.

At the club the music was reaching sweet and hot. Joe and I parked our coats and waited for the girls. In a little while Maxie walked toward us alone. Her cheeks were very red, her eyes looked layer-on-layer with little lights. She was still mad at me.

I went up to her, leaving Joe behind. "Come on,

kid," I pleaded gently. "Let's link arms and let go and forget we're Oscar's parents. This is the feast of St. Valentine."

She didn't say anything. But she let me put my arms around her and we were off, smooth as silk and intricate as a maze, the way we'd always danced.

It was good, if silent, fun. We stayed together for two dances and an encore, then I let a stag cut in and went to find Pamela.

It was some time before I discovered her. She was coming in the door from the porch with Joe. The first thing I thought, numbly, was that she had the look of a girl who has just been thoroughly and satisfactorily kissed.

The second thing stopped me dead in my tracks. As in a nightmare I watched the beautiful tall figure waft gracefully toward me. My horrified eyes held on her shoulder. It got larger and more lifelike as it drew closer. When they stood before me I felt as if my eyes were saucers and my mouth a soup plate.

Fastened to the slim strap of Pamela's white dress was my heart-shaped corsage, bow and all. But it had been pinned, none too precisely, smack dab in the middle of a bouncing corsage of pink sweet peas.

Some things make you ill. Each person gets ill from a different cause. I thought for a moment I was going to disgrace myself in front of everybody. But I guess I didn't show it.

Because Pamela said, "I didn't know which to wear, Larry." She looked proud. Actually proud. "I really couldn't decide, and I didn't want to hurt your feelings. So...I just put them together." She lifted her face to Joe's. The just-kissed look came back. She touched the sweetheart roses tenderly.

I opened my mouth. Then I was aware of Maxie's hand, pinching my ear, playfully but intensely, as it had so many times before. "Let's dance, Squirt," she said lightly.

"I—I—"

"Right now," she commanded in a terse whisper. "This very minute, before you start yelling, or get any greener."

I let her push me away a foot or so. Pamela's voice stopped me again.

"I do want to thank you, Larry," she said. "Your sweet peas are just too pretty for words."

I looked at Pamela, tall and cool and lovely. I looked up at Joe, red-faced and almost pleading. I didn't look at Maxie. But a little pulsating something went out from me to her. I took a deep breath and swallowed.

"I'm glad you like them, Pam," I managed to say casually. "They...they sort of reminded me of you."

Joe's eyes loosened with relief. *Pal,* they thanked.

You can do a lot of thinking while your feet move skilfully and automatically in time to music. I thought. "They sort of reminded me of you," I'd said. Insipid. Sweet peas. Mashed potatoes. Macaroni. No sense of humor. Cards on a mirror.

I looked at Maxie's head, which reached so blessedly just to my mouth. I felt how comfortable my arm was around her waist. I saw her hand on my shoulder, with little red spots where it had caught on thorns. I thought of the months I was away, and business kept up fine, and Maxie laughing at me, and taking care of Oscar.

I pulled her closer. She lifted her head. There was a sort of sleepy look in her eyes. There was a very slight, carefully covered redness around them. As if her crying of the morning had gone on for a long time.

"It's just that...she isn't a florist, Larry. She didn't know how it would look to you. She thinks Joe—"

"Hush," I said. "Put your head back. Finish this dance without a word." I put my cheek against her hair. Maybe it looked wild sometimes. But it felt very soft. A dark sweet soft.

When three uplifted notes signaled intermission, I took Maxie to a chair. I sat her there.

"Stay right here," I ordered. "Don't move. Don't dance with anybody else. Stay right in this spot until I get back. I'll be back in exactly one half hour."

She nodded. It wasn't until I was racing the car down Main Street that I realized how meek and feminine and inefficient her nod had been. It made me feel swell.

At first my fingers were all thumbs, working against time that way. But in a few minutes they snapped out of it and sort of turned inspired. I was through with eight minutes left to get back to the club.

Maxie sat there, her hands folded in her lap like a good girl. The sophisticated black dress didn't make any difference. She was a good little girl.

I stood in front of her. I took her hand with my free one. I led her to the glassed-in porch. It was sprayed with bands of light and dark from the windows of the dance room. I pushed her to a dark band.

"You said," I whispered, and my throat was raw as with tonsillitis, and Pam had never set my heart to pumping as it was, "you said nobody ever sends you flowers."

I could feel her, so still. For Maxie, so very still and waiting. I pulled her over into a band of light. I took my hand from behind me. I held it out like a stick of candy.

"Oh, Squirt," she murmured. "Oh, Squirt. It's Oscar."

"He's for you," I said softly. "He's always been for you. You made him grow. He was sort of stubborn about it, but he had sense enough at last—" I stopped, praying she would understand.

"Oh, Squirt," she said again. She understood, all right.

"And don't call me Squirt," I commanded absent-mindedly. I bent to kiss her. I leaned down to kiss Maxie.

After a long time she pulled me into the dark band of the porch again. "Oh, Squirt," she insisted.

I could barely hear her. But then, she didn't have a chance to repeat it, anyhow.

Maxie and I have been a pair of beavers these past three days. Pam and Joe are getting married and it's a big showy all-out affair. Pam asked me to do the flowers.

I sputtered about it. "A lot of wasted effort," I complained. "No matter how I knock myself out, the dame won't appreciate it. She has no taste."

Maxie came over and kissed me, a habit of newly-weds even during business hours. "She has no taste," she agreed. And she looked right at me when she said it.

LOVE
IS TOO
YOUNG

My daughter stands before me and she is so beautiful my breath halts around my heart. Her dark red hair curls softly and her cheeks are high and round at the same time. There is such clarity to her skin, such a mixture of all shades in her eyes, such a fullness and warmth to her lips, that I shudder a little for the youngness of her.

She frowns at me and moves, long legged and easy, around the big room.

"Mother," she says, and her voice is good, low and precise, the way she has been taught. "Mother, you just don't understand." The sentence echoes around the room. At first it doesn't touch me. But finally it reaches my ears and slaps against my face as sharply as if it were my daughter's hand.

"Darling," I find myself saying, "look around you." I swing my hand to include the gracious room, the deep windows, the heavy draperies, the huge fireplace. "This is all part of you. It's what you have been brought up in. Just like your clothes, your car, the Swiss school, your friends—"

She shakes her head and her mouth is held tight. I

don't look above it, afraid to see tears in her eyes. Since she was small I couldn't bear to see the way she held the tears dammed against her lashes, too proud to let them fall.

"Your father and I," I begin again, "we want everything the very best for you. From the beginning it's been our dream, the thing your father has worked for...."

Her mouth softens. "I know," she says. For a moment we are close again, as we haven't been these past two months. "But he—he is the best, mother."

I know she doesn't mean her father. For the boy, she says "he" as if his name were too precious to share with us.

I shake my head, unable to stop.

It bursts out of her then. "You don't see, do you? You don't understand. You're not young enough, not tolerant enough. Things. They're what you think are important. Junk." She flips her hand out, refuting possessions.

Anger stirs in me, slowly at first, then flares to match the blaze in her eyes.

"That is quite enough of that," I say firmly. "It's obvious this boy has already made his mark on you. It's clear that he can never reach your standards, so he is pulling you down to his. A three-room apartment in a dingy part of town, then a cheap row house, babies one after another, scrimping and worrying—"

She tilts back her head and laughs.

"Phooey," she cries. "There's no use. We're a million miles apart. A row house with him would be heaven." She stops and looks at me. "Will be heaven, and there's not one single thing you can do to stop me."

She swings around. She runs from the room and the pat of her flat slippers whispers up the stairs.

I am alone.

After a while it begins to get dark. I don't turn on the lights. I sit by the window. In the purple of the dusk I see my daughter go out the front door, climb into the waiting jalopy, sit close to the broad shoulders of the boy. I hear, from a distance, the roar and start of the engine.

If only her father hadn't gone to Washington. If he were just here this time when she has brought it out into the open. Perhaps he would know what to say.

They will ride around, the two of them, and she will tell this stranger, this blunt young man who has known poverty and Korea and working in gas stations to pay for his schooling, she will tell him about her mother. As if I was an enemy. I put back my head and close my eyes.

Love is a one-way street, I think. And she walks down it quickly, eagerly, not knowing that the pavement ends with a yellow sign and big black letters, Dead End. Not knowing that to retrace her steps, now or at any time, will be a long, heartbreaking hike with a destination certain to be full of grief.

I remember the day Jerry first came to the house. He stood under the pillars and he looked small, although he was tall enough, a good deal taller than Jan was.

There was a party going on in the house. Young people were all over and the record player was making music for their dancing. Helga, the maid, was carrying trays in among them, smiling and joking.

When the bell rang, Jan said, "I'll take it, Helga. Johnny over there is going to fall flat from starvation if you don't give him a sandwich." She ran across the wide room and down the broad hall and opened the door. The boy was there.

"Hello," he said. His voice sounded choked in his throat and thin, as if it had just changed, although he was 21 and normally spoke in a sure way.

"Why, hello," Jan said. She couldn't account for it, the funny way her pulses shook. "What are you doing here?"

"I was just passing by," Jerry said, as if he walked the three miles from town every day on his way home. "You said, 'Come see me sometime,' remember?"

Jan smiled and reached out a hand, the way she had been taught. "Of course," she agreed. "Come in. There's a brawl going on, but we can always stand an extra man."

He pulled back from her hand. "I wouldn't want to crash anything. Some other time."

She went after him and touched his sleeve. Her fingers prickled suddenly. In a shaft of late-afternoon sun between the pillars, his eyes were very blue.

"I want you to meet everybody," she said.

They went in together through the big door.

Jan was always one for feeling atmosphere. She knew, as they stood before her friends, what they were thinking and seeing.

They were thinking, *Where did Jan find this?* They were seeing the way the boy's hair curled a little too long, as if he put as much time as possible between haircuts; the small darns in his clean gray sweater; the shine of his navy blue trousers; the thinness, almost fraying, of his white collar.

"This is Jerry," she cried brightly.

Then she forgot about them and shared the way Jerry lifted his square chin and swallowed hard. The way he curled inside of himself, more aware than all of them of his shabbiness.

She linked her arm through his and walked him from one guest to another. Then someone put on a new record and Helga stood before them, in the corner by the grand piano, with her tray extended and a grin on her face.

"Take two, they're small," she said. The boy did look hungry, as if he would eat because he needed to and not just for fun.

"No, thank you," Jerry said. He smiled at her and they were friends. They knew each other, he and

Helga. They knew how it was to serve people and to try to please them, to say, "Yes, sir," and "Yes, ma'am." They knew he couldn't take a sandwich because he wanted one.

Jan sat down on the piano bench. She felt a little weak, as if she had gone too many lengths of the pool.

"Sit down," she said, patting the space beside her.

Jerry sat down carefully. "Nice joint," he said, staring around, making his voice deliberately coarse. "I didn't realize, those times in the store, that you were so well-heeled."

Jan tried to laugh. "Not me," she said. "My mother and father. They brought me up."

"But for all practical purposes—"

"For all practical purposes," she agreed, "if you like such things...." *Treason,* her mind cried. *You, who loves your pretty room, your pretty clothes. Treason.*

Jerry swung around the end of the bench and put his feet under the piano. He reached out a hand and touched the keys gently. Jan looked at his hand, clean, broad through the middle, with square nails and strong fingers.

"Do you play?" she asked him.

He nodded. "A little. By ear."

His fingers began to move, slowly, softly, making a counterpoint to the louder record music. Jan could tell that he tried to keep it soft but it ran away with him. His foot began to beat against the rug. In no time the hot, shouting music filled the room.

Somebody turned off the record player. They moved in around the piano. They leaned and listened.

Jan felt their breathing. But mostly she was aware of the breathing beside her, the hum that came out softly from Jerry's lips. Once he turned to look at her. The way he smiled changed his face completely.

When they all decided to go, she went to the door with them. She stood there, saying good-night. She said, "Glad you had a good time."

She smiled when the girls leaned to whisper, "What a man! He's perfectly darling."

All the time, with the cool night air pushing in toward her and her guests leaving, Jan was listening to the piano music, slow now and tender, "Night and Day...."

She shut the door slowly and stood staring at its panels for a long moment, remembering.

"I'll get the groceries today, Helga," she'd said, when was it? Two weeks ago?

She took the car and left it to be greased and walked to the biggest grocery store in town. Jerry was there, stretching to the top shelves, smiling at her.

"Come again," he said that first time, carrying the bag of groceries to the door for her. "Please come again," he repeated as she started down the street.

"I'll get the groceries today, Helga," she said the next time. Then she and Helga took it for granted and never said anything. But Jan knew that Helga knew somehow, and three mornings a week Helga, grinning a little, handed her the list.

Now Jan knew that Jerry's last name was Sims. That his father had been a minister in the next town. That Jerry took care of his mother. That he had finished one year of college before his father died. That his mother took in a little sewing, not much, because she had trouble with her eyes.

Six times to the store then, and slow selection of purchases and the walk to the door with the big brown bag in Jerry's strong arms.

"Come and see me sometime."

Now she turned away from a door again, only this time toward the music, toward Jerry Sims.

She sat down beside him. His breath picked up a tempo the music didn't have. He played and there was no knowing how long it was. Only suddenly her mother and father were there, back from their party.

"This is Jerry Sims, mother," Jan said, jumping to her feet.

The music stopped abruptly and Jerry stood beside her. It was strange, the way the two of them seemed aligned, facing her parents.

Her parents didn't try to be polite.

"Where are the others?" her father asked.

"You'll excuse us," her mother said. "It's getting very late."

Jan searched her mother's eyes. There was a wariness in them as they examined Jerry Sims. Jerry looked back at her steadily.

"I'll be going," he said.

Jan's mother nodded and her eyes relaxed a little bit. "It was nice to meet you," she said, as if Jerry was about to take a train out of town with a no-return ticket.

Jan's father put out his hand and shook Jerry's briefly. "Goodbye," he said with matching finality.

"Good night, sir," Jerry said.

They stood, watching her parents cross the room, her mother twitching a drapery, turning out a lamp. Framed in the outside door, Jerry said, "I get Thursday afternoons off."

Jan said, "Tomorrow is Thursday."

They nodded at each other solemnly.

She put out her hand, not knowing why, and it went into Jerry's as if it belonged there. She felt the tightening of his fingers, the tensing of his arm muscles, as he began to pull her toward him. Then her father's voice called from the head of the stairs.

"Jan, bring up my book, will you? It's on the coffee table. And come along yourself."

She slipped her hand from Jerry's. So that's how it was going to be. Her father, who had never hurried off one of her friends before.

"Tomorrow," she whispered to Jerry. "I'll meet you at the store."

They were conspirators. They were together, more
closely than if he had pulled her against him and
kissed her. He nodded. Then he turned around
abruptly and strode across the porch. In a moment his
whistle came, the familiar notes of "Night and Day."

She had sandwiches and the car Thursday at noon.
Jerry came out, hurrying and jumped in beside her.

"It's warm," Jan said. "I thought maybe the peninsula?"

He lounged back in the seat. "I didn't bring swim
trunks."

She smiled. "I did. One of dad's."

He didn't look at her.

"Crazy thing," he said almost to himself. "All the
way home last night I kept saying over and over to
myself, 'That's my girl. There's my girl.'" He shook
his head.

Jan held the wheel very carefully.

"It was crazy, wasn't it?" he asked.

"I don't see why," she managed.

He snorted. "She doesn't see why. How much did
this car cost?"

"It belongs to my father."

She turned right, off the mainland, and the big car
moved onto the narrow finger of the peninsula. The
bay sparkled and Johnny's boat was out there.

She thought of this morning's phone call. "I'm
sorry, Johnny, I can't go sailing today. Something has
come up."

"A certain muscle-bound peasant, by any chance?"
Johnny inquired, all the usual pleasantness gone from
his voice. "I'll outsit him. I'll outlast him. Maybe I
can't fight him but I'll insult him to death—"

She'd hung up on him and now there was his boat.
She looked away. The lake stretched forever blue and
the sand was very white. She drove until the peninsula
widened to include bushes and then trees.

"Here?" she asked Jerry.

"Here," he agreed, breaking his long quiet.

They ate on a rock that jutted into a wooded inlet of the lake. They were still most of the time.

What Jan felt then she had never felt before. It frightened her. In a sudden spurt they would both begin to speak. It was funny. They laughed.

After a while Jerry went into the bushes. When he came out he had on her father's bathing suit. It was too big and that was funny, too. Only Jerry wasn't funny. He was beautiful, as a 21-year-old man can be beautiful. From playing kickball and swimming and stretching to unload groceries. She jumped to her feet, unbuttoning the cotton dress she wore over her suit, running quickly across the sand, hearing the pounding of Jerry's bare feet behind her. She swam fast. Yet with all her racing there was the prayer that Jerry, despite her best efforts, would catch up with her.

He did. He came up behind her and put his hands on her shoulders, and they were big enough to cup the bone and the brown flesh completely. He swung her around, the two of them treading water rhythmically, and the hands were inexorable, pulling her toward him, until their lips were together.

When Jan opened her eyes, he was no longer touching her. He was instead swimming with too much splashing farther into the lake.

She lay on her back, looking up at a cloud moving alone in the sky.

"I'm sorry." Jerry's voice came beside her.

She moved her head a little. He was floating, too, the two of them lying on the water in a strange sort of intimacy.

"Why?" she asked.

He laughed and treaded water.

"'Why?' the girl asks. 'Why not?' she asks." He shook his head and little drops of water sprayed side-wise from his wet hair. "There are reasons for things,

Jan. I shouldn't think, 'There is my girl.' I shouldn't kiss you." All the laughter left his face. "Only I've wanted to. Every time you've come into the store."

The water under Jan was a cloud, like the one she had been staring at. She felt it puff and float and somehow get inside of her so that she was all happiness.

"Why?" she asked, this time on a laugh.

"Because I love you," he said. "I love you."

She turned in the water, all pulses and heartbeat, and swam quickly toward the shore. On the sand she waited, tall and proud, for Jerry to stand before her. Waited for him to kiss her again, to hold her.

But he didn't. He walked straight past her to the bushes. It seemed a very long time before he came out, fully dressed.

"Let's go," he said brusquely.

They drove in silence. When they turned off the peninsula she said, "I can see I'm going to have trouble with you."

Then in a sudden reversal of mood, they pulled back their heads and let the laughter roll out. Until finally Jan stopped the car under a broad tree beside the road, and the laughter died because their lips were so close, so touching, that there wasn't room for it. Only room for emotions infinitely bigger than laughter.

"I love you, too," Jan said solidly, at last.

She started the car and drove back to the store. When she stopped, Jerry sat still for a moment. "I'll be through at nine o'clock," he said.

"I can't see you tonight."

"Why not? One of those—those others?"

Jan shook her head. "We're having a dinner party—mother and dad, I mean."

He opened the door. "Dinner party," he echoed quietly. His mouth was tight again. "See what I mean? Before my father died we'd ask folks in to supper. My mother's never had a dinner party in her life."

"There's no harm in calling it dinner."

"No harm at all," Jerry said coldly. He got out of the car and walked blindly toward the store. Jan slid out after him quickly.

"Jerry," she called, trying to keep it soft, feeling the nervousness and intensity of it all through her. "Jerry, please."

He turned back toward her as quickly as he had turned away. "Darling," he whispered.

They nodded at each other. Then Jan got back in the car and started the engine.

All the way home she felt more grown up than she ever had in her life.

"It will be all right, Jerry," she murmured to herself. "Everything will turn out fine."

That night she waited on the steps of the front porch, sitting quietly in the dark, watching the way the shadows down the path lay softly, waiting for the deeper shadow that would be Jerry Sims.

When he came, they walked together around to the side yard. They sat there, holding hands. Jerry talked. He told her about his mother and how it had to be with him, and studying insurance at night.

When he was through, Jan used the same confident words she had told herself that afternoon. They seemed to be the right ones, because Jerry believed her.

Her father's voice came to them, suddenly near. "Jan, are you out there?"

She stood up quickly, smoothing her hair. "Here, dad," she said.

In the dim light her father came closer, peering. "Johnny with you?" he asked. Then, "Oh, it's you, young man."

Jerry said. "Yes, sir." He turned to Jan. "I'll have to go now. Grocery stores open at seven, you know. I'll

see you. I'll call you." He nodded at Jan's father and
circled him.

"Good night, Jerry," Jan called. "Good night. I'll
see you tomorrow."

"Oh no, you won't," her father whispered.

"Oh yes, I will," Jan whispered back.

It was a final declaration of war.

She ran past him, to the back of the house, to
Helga's solid arms.

"They can't stop us, can they, Helga?"

Helga patted her and gave her a dish towel to wipe
her eyes. "They won't want to, once they understand," she comforted. "Never did see two people set
such a store on one girl."

But that's just it, Jan thought forlornly, tiptoeing up
the back stairs. *That's just it, exactly.*

A summer like that one, everything squeezes together
like an accordion. You can pull it out later, maybe,
when you're older and have time to look at all the
ridges. But when you're young and it's happening, the
music is so loud and fast, the accordion ripples open
and shut in such a hurry, that you hear it and see it
only in glimpses.

Oh, they were happy, Jan and her boy Jerry Sims.
They stayed away from the big house as much as
possible, away from people who would spoil things.
They walked the tangled places of the peninsula and
miles down the white sand. They climbed the hills
behind the town. They talked endlessly.

Every word was a pledge they both heard. Of hope.
Of the plans they evolved.

"We'll take what money we have saved. Not much,
but it's a start," Jerry would say.

"I can work, too, you know. I'm not completely
stupid," Jan would rush in.

"And we'll go to the city and find us a couple of
rooms."

They would be quiet then, thinking of a couple of rooms that were all their own. It was a very big thought. A couple of rooms with a door that would shut and a key that would turn.

Until one afternoon in late summer.

"I can't believe we really have to go away," Jan said. "I can't believe my family won't understand if we both talk to them."

For a moment, saying it, she meant it completely. Then the sureness went out of her.

"What's wrong with him?" she had cried to her father the night before. "Why can't you remember his name? Why do you call him 'that young man' as if he was a—a criminal?"

"There's nothing wrong with him," her father had said, not even lifting his face from the paper, "for some nice poor young girl who knows how to make do. Nothing wrong with him, in his proper place."

"You can hurt him, too, you know, Jan," her mother added. "When you go away to school—"

I'm not going away anywhere, Jan thought. But she didn't say it. There was something so sure and quiet about the two of them.

"Better tell him not to come around again," her father said, this time looking up, nodding his head, making it, however softly said, a command.

"I'll tell him," Jan had found herself saying furiously. "I'll tell him I'm born of a couple of snobs who think money is everything." She began to cry and ran from the room.

She didn't tell him. She was going to. This late-summer afternoon she intended to. But Jerry said it first.

"Quit dreaming," he said fiercely. "We'll never go away. The only place I could take you is home to my mother. I can't leave her. I wouldn't want to. She's worth 10 of your kind of people."

"Jerry," Jan whispered, but he didn't hear.

"And how do you think she feels?" He glared at her. "Oh, she knows about you. So do all her friends and neighbors. They think I'm making a fool of myself. People like us, we have our pride, too."

"Jerry, listen," Jan tried again, pushing back the tears that bounced to her eyes.

"So, we have a big scene with your folks. We walk out. We get married. There we are, cozy, the three of us, and my mother will be nice to you. But she'll feel small, apologizing for the old furniture and not having shiny pans to cook in and nothing fancy to cook in them."

He couldn't seem to stop. Jan stopped trying to make him. She sat quietly crying, as if the world around her had blown up and there was nothing she could do but weep for it.

"Sure, someday I'll try to sell insurance. At night, after I've worked in the store all day. How would you like that? Sitting around every night with my mother while I try to make an extra buck? And no pretty clothes and all your friends sorry for you—" He ran down suddenly.

Jan reached for his hand. He pulled it away.

"I love you," she said.

He shook his head. "Well," he said slowly in a voice she had never heard before, "that's too bad for you. But you'll get over it."

"You love me," she said.

He stood up. He shook his head again. "Not enough. Not anywhere near enough to stand the gaff. I never knew a girl like you before, that's all. I—I got mixed up."

Suddenly there was no pride at all in Jan. There was just a wild fear that seemed to block the flow of all thought.

"Jerry," she cried loudly. She jumped up. She put her arms around him. She put her mouth against his.

"Jerry," she whispered. "Please, please, please."

His arms stayed at his sides, and his mouth didn't move against hers.

Even through the wildness, through the tears, the thought that she was trying to hold, was trying to kiss, a boy who refused to respond, managed to etch its way into her mind. It pushed her away from Jerry, straightened her shoulders and dried her eyes.

"Brother," she said clearly, "was I ever mistaken about you." She shrugged. "Don't worry about me. It's not going to be a bit hard to forget you, Jerry Sims. I never did have much use for cowards." She switched herself around. Over her shoulder she added, "Or liars. Or cheats." Then she ran.

It was a long run down the hill. It was a long run across the back fields toward home, and the sight of the house was like the sight of outstretched arms.

She ran frantically through the door. Her father was in the big chair by the window.

"You were right," she cried to him. "You were absolutely right. I hate him and he's not worth anybody's little finger."

She couldn't turn around fast enough to avoid seeing the mingled look of relief and concern in her father's eyes.

She went directly to her room. Then the pain came in on her and there couldn't be such pain. There couldn't exist such an agony of heart, of mind, of all sources that couldn't be touched or healed.

Through it she heard her mother's voice. "It happened to me once, darling," her mother was saying, her words growing loud and soft, loud and soft. "Puppy love," her mother said. "We all go through it and are almost always better for it."

"Go away," Jan whispered. "Go away."

When the door shut softly, she made herself sit up. She made herself realize that it wasn't going to get better. That she loved Jerry Sims. Now, always, with no puppy love in it.

She went to her closet and grabbed a coat. She had to go to him. She moved toward the door but it pushed inward.

Helga stood there, one finger on her lips. "He's in the kitchen," she whispered. "Back in the breakfast nook. You get down there."

There was no hallway, no stairs, no transition. Jan was just suddenly standing in the breakfast nook and Jerry was getting to his feet. Once on them, he swayed a little, as if he had been drinking or was ill.

"Jan," he said thickly, "I can't stand it."

Who moved first, Jan never knew. The things she knew were so great, so permanent, that she only pushed herself warmly against Jerry, her head on his shoulder. There were no kisses. Just the holding and the warmth and the knowing.

Jerry's voice came out firmly at last, the one she knew. I'll get every single thing for you," he said, and it sounded like a marriage vow. "A house as fine as this and everything. Every single thing."

Jan tried to shake her head, but he was holding her too closely for any movement.

It doesn't matter, she tried to say. *Nothing matters but us,* she wanted to tell him. She couldn't. She knew he had to make that vow.

"Heaven in a breakfast nook," she managed to murmur instead.

I get up suddenly in the dark room. I do not turn on a light.

Instead, I walk eagerly toward the door and open it and step onto the broad porch with its thick white pillars. I stare out across the wide tended lawn toward the street. I can feel my head tip to listen. For the sound of a jalopy, for the noise of its slammed door and the shuffle of my daughter's slippers up the walk.

I am attuned, all vibration. I don't want my daughter to come up that walk. I want to beat her to it. I want to run down to her.

I want to put my arm around her waist and reach up my other hand to the boy's shoulder. I want to kiss my daughter and then kiss the boy's flat cheek above his square jaw.

I want to say, and the words are clear in my mind, "I understand, kids. I understand every single bit of it. Every wonderful step of that one-way street. I understand."

But underneath my listening, there is another waiting. A deeper one, a wilder one. I want the cab to come. The cab that will bring my husband from the airport, from the insurance conference in Washington.

And when he has come up the steps and set his bag down and cleared his throat the way he does before he says things, I want to go to him and reach for him and cling to him.

I want to kiss him and then I want to say, "I love you. I love you, Jerry."

Life being what it is, I haven't said it in a long time. Jerry, being what he is, he'll know what I mean, all that I mean.

Funny, it doesn't matter which one of them comes home first. I have the same message for both of them, my daughter and my husband.

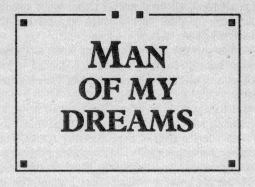

MAN OF MY DREAMS

Came one of those days when Clara Hodson particularly loved the great department store called Helderson's. Although it was spring, something about it spoke of Christmas. The lights that glittered on the silverware, the long clean-swept aisles, the well-dressed people, the feeling that here under one roof were collected treasures and hidden joys.

She hated peanuts, though. Because she did, she hurried the pouring of them out into small mountains on the center counter, before the thick salty smell could really get to her.

"Ten billion, four hundred and seventeen, at least," she muttered to herself.

By eleven o'clock she had sold fourteen pounds of them and six neckties. It was quite a trick, going from the greasy nuts to the silken scarves without transferring the residue of one to the spotlessness of the other. "Marie," she said to the girl across the aisle, "tend the rubbish heap, will you, while I clean up my hands?"

Marie was contrasty, black and white and red, with white shining teeth that she had used for dazzling. "Sure thing, Sis," she called.

Clara slid out from the counter with a little sigh. Marie always made her feel pastel, pink nails, pale yellow hair, light blue eyes, plain gray dress. Shy as a rabbit, she thought disgustedly, compared to Marie.

She started down the aisle toward Mr. Drake, who paced the narrow byways of Helderson's, his cuffs extending slightly from the sleeves. She felt a little hidden shake inside of her. Floorwalkers were natural enemies. A new floorwalker, whose coming had kept the main floor buzzing for a week, was a special hazard. Something about this one bothered Clara, so that she found herself peeking covertly at him whenever she wasn't busy.

"Good morning, Mr. Drake," she said thinly.

Ronald Drake looked downed at her. He bowed. "Miss Hodson," he stated flatly.

Clara focused on his left ear. "I'd like to take my time out," she said and felt a hot dryness on her cheeks. With old Mr. Adams, now, the phrase seemed natural. With young Mr. Drake it sort of strangled her.

Mr. Drake jotted down her name on the slip of paper he carried with him. "Very well."

Marie had called him a stuffed shirt. Staring at his ear that way, Clara noted that the hair at the back of his neck was blonder than the rest and that it was exactly the same pale shade as her own.

She had started to turn away when Mr. Drake's formal voice stopped her. "Miss Hodson," he began and cleared his throat.

She swung back. "Yes, sir?"

"I..." He hesitated. "I think you're doing very well. I've been watching you."

Surprise swiveled her glance to his eyes. They were really amazingly blue. "You have?"

He nodded. "And I have been wondering—" his hands flipped the pages of the small notebook "—perhaps if you are free some evening...perhaps we could have dinner together?"

He left it there. It stayed there for quite a breathless period of time. Mr. Drake, the floorwalker! Clara swallowed hard.

"Why, yes," she managed at last. "Why...yes."

"Tonight?" he asked.

Clara nodded, speechless.

He poised his pencil again. "Your address?"

It was like applying for a job. She told him.

"Seven all right?"

She nodded again, then, suddenly overcome with it all, she swung around and hastened to the employees' elevator.

A kind of story that Clara Hodson always liked to read began with a cocktail party. Not that she took anything herself, of course. When you're brought up to enjoy cold frosty milk and homemade doughnuts, cocktails and those little snacks that look as if they had died in the middle of writhing hold no special appeal.

No, it wasn't the cocktails. It was the crowded room, just like the song. And there she was, the girl who was the heroine, tall and sleek, her crisp dress flared around her or her moss-green suit all slim lines, her hair gleaming under a tiny hat with a mischievous veil. There she was with a group of people, gaily chatting by the window.

There he was, the hero, way across the room by the fireplace, his broad shoulders easy under hand-tailored tweeds, his fine brown fingers holding the slim stem of a shining glass, his glance restless on the pretty girls who laughed up at him.

Then it happened. Then his eyes strayed, stopped, lighted, met those of the tall girl in the crisp dress or the green suit, and held. The room grew still around them. It was as if they were alone on a desert island. He found himself moving slowly, bucking the tide of gay idle people, a man with a destination. He came up to her and her eyes looked evenly at him under the small veil. He set his glass down and said in a deep soft voice, "Let's get out of here."

They did. They knew. Right away and at once, they knew. It didn't matter where they went from there, what adventures opened out to them in the story; the tale had begun right, with a flare, with excitement, with promise.

No matter how many times Clara Hodson read that beginning, and there were plenty of times, she always felt a quick little tickle around the region of her heart. Whether she was reading in bed, in the beauty shop, or looking at the stacks of magazines in the store cafeteria at noon, she always searched first for stories that began that way.

Marie had opinions about reading. "There's more romance in Roseland, Sis, than you'll ever find in your stories."

Clara always nodded. "For you, sure," she agreed, admiring Marie's brilliance, her blatancy. "You just walk into the place and all the men see you."

She'd tried Roseland once. It was quite an ordeal to make herself go. But Roseland was a crowded room and perhaps he would be there, to see her standing hesitantly in the doorway.

He wasn't, of course. She had a few dances with Marie's left-over friends but she didn't try it again.

She did pretty well on her own, for a quiet girl, a pastel girl. Three of the clerks in Helderson's alternated to see that her Saturday nights were filled. If they were filled with spaghetti (cheap at Lonzo's) and the movies (cheap at neighborhood theaters) she understood perfectly and asked nothing more.

So Clara Hodson stared into the mirror in the employees' lounge and thought of romance and of Ronald Drake and tried to fit him into it. Marie would hoot and pull her voice down to a precise facsimile of Mr. Drake's. She would clear her throat in his way and end on a burst of laughter. "Oh, Clara," she would scream, "not that fuddy-duddy!"

He seems like a very nice young man, Clara answered Marie defensively, if silently.

She tried to fit him into her dream beginning. She couldn't make it jell at all. He wasn't tall enough, nor dark enough, nor eager enough. That hero across a crowded room would never clear his throat before his murmured, "Let's get out of here."

She sighed and went back to her peanuts.

The church bell across the street was on the third stroke of seven when the switchboard girl rang Clara's room and said, "There's a caller here for you." Clara couldn't tell from her voice whether she though Ronald Drake was a stuffed shirt or not.

Clara straightened the skirt of her new black and purple dress and walked down the wide old stairs.

Ronald Drake paced in his off hours, too. He wore a light gray suit and a pale yellow tie.

"Good evening," Clara said and he turned.

"Miss Hodson," he said, nodding.

It was exactly as if she were asking for her time-off period. A giggle started nervously on its way but she managed to check it and turn it into the word, "Ready?"

"Ready," he agreed. "My car is outside."

It was a small neat gray car. It looked as brushed and careful as Mr. Drake.

"I thought perhaps you might like to dine at the Moon Roof," he said.

Dine, Clara thought, the pompous word tickling against her throat. "I've never actually dined," she wanted to say. "Usually I just eat." Then "Moon Roof" registered and she felt her breath catch. It was elegant and smooth and very expensive and even Marie had never been there.

"We could go to a—a simpler place," she offered.

He had a way of pushing out his chin. "Not at all," he said firmly. "If you'd enjoy it, of course."

"Oh, I certainly would," Clara breathed.

Clara wasn't so sure about the extent of her enjoyment when they stepped off the elevator, the sound of their feet hushed by thick carpets. She was suddenly and uncomfortably aware of the simplicity of her tailored dress and the contrasting pink tulle of the cocktail dress preceding them.

Ronald Drake seemed quite at ease, though. He spoke definitely to the headwaiter, took Clara's arm, saw that she was settled at the white-covered table and picked up the wine list as if he knew every vintage. Clara gave him a weak little smile at his considered suggestion and hoped that it looked intelligent. Then she let her glance move around the room.

It was a beautiful room, filled with a moon glow that looked almost authentic, so that the tables with their candles looked silvery white. The women's dresses were brilliant pompons against their neutrality, the men's dark suits sharp accents, exciting and dashing.

"This is wonderful." She smiled at him.

"I'm glad that you like it," he said. He didn't clear his throat.

"Do you come here often?" Clara asked.

He looked embarrassed. "As a matter of fact," he admitted, "this is the first time. My roommate, the fellow I share an apartment with, recommended it."

Silence dropped. They both sat watching the fairyland world. The waiter came and deftly poured two glasses of amber wine. Clara welcomed the break in the quiet. Maybe after she drank the wine she could think of something to say. She wasn't used to wine. It was supposed to make you sparkle, wasn't it?

Ronald Drake lifted his glass. He cleared his throat. "I ordered this wine," he said, "because it reminds me of the color of your hair. Almost exactly."

Clara stared and felt her mouth begin to drop. A hard bright flush filled his cheeks, as if he hadn't meant to say it, as if it had slipped out from his thoughts. She felt an identical blush begin to heat her own face.

She took a quick swallow of the wine. "How do you like working at Helderson's?" she asked.

"I like it very much." The flush began to calm itself. "It's a fine store, good reputation, good place to get ahead..."

The waiter came and put something strange and delicious before them. Clara dipped daintily into it, alternating her gaze from the concoction to Ronald Drake's face, smiling in the right places, letting him know that she, too, thought Helderson's a fine place to work. All the time she waited for the wine to do its reputed job. To put bright witty words on her lips and gaiety in the tilt of her chin. *Apparently,* she thought wistfully, *the power of wine is much overrated.* In any case, it didn't matter too much, because he kept talking about Helderson's all through the next course.

Now it's my turn, Clara thought, and took a deep breath. "Do you like to dance?" she asked abruptly.

He looked suddenly unhappy. "I should have thought of it," he apologized.

Clara shook her head. It hadn't come out the way she meant it. It sounded like a hint, as if she were restless. He got up and took her arm. They made a path through the tables and out onto the crowded floor.

Ronald Drake, Clara thought, was an adequate if uninspired dancer. He danced the way he walked the floors at Helderson's and drove his car. Strictly on the beat, with no inventions, nothing to startle. But his arms were surprisingly strong and firmly muscled.

When the music stopped and they were back at their table, Clara felt breathless and excited. Dancing always did that to her.

He was saying, "Let's have something outstanding for dessert."

Clara cried happily, "Oh, let's."

For a long moment he stared at her, as if he had forgotten dessert or was suddenly confused. Clara found herself staring, too, with only one thought in her: that his eyes were the bluest she had ever seen. Then the shyness hit and they broke the gaze.

Clara turned toward the room. Her eyes lighted at once on a tall figure at the top of the steps leading into the dining room. He stood there, commandingly somehow, casually taking in the complete scene. He had a lean brown face, thick dark hair, and even from that distance, she saw, eyes as black as night.

Clara watched him, fascinated. Her heart began to pound in a beat-thud that was stronger than when she read the stories. Time held, each moment counted out by her heart, while he scanned the orchestra, the tables by the window, the tables in the center of the room, and swung his gaze slowly, with a feeling of destination, toward the right side, past the pillars, to the corner where she sat.

It happened. Oh, she knew it would and it did. The somber look went away from his mouth. It turned up brilliantly and his long legs put themselves into action. He moved gracefully and with purpose down the steps. His arms swung a little, his gaze stayed steady and he walked toward her, straight as if he had been searching for a long time to find her just exactly where she was.

It was a suspended moment. Through it she heard Ronald Drake's voice. "Are you all right, Clara? You look so strange."

Clara smiled abstractedly.

He said, "I've asked you twice if you would like the baked Alaska."

The man was closer now, so close she could see how very white his teeth were. She couldn't think any more, because she was all feeling, all quick irregular breathing. The man was upon them. He wasn't going past. He wasn't stopping at the table to the left nor the right. He was beside their table. He was leaning forward, his eyes darker than even she had believed possible, and focused on her, right on her, with intensity in them and a promise of laughter too. His arm reached out, then his hand came down and landed solidly on Ronald Drake's shoulder.

"Ronald," he cried (what a rich warm voice). "Good old Ronald! Imagine finding you here."

"Just imagine," Ronald said flatly, "seeing as how I told you just before I left, Craig."

Craig, Clara thought. A wonderful name.

"And this is the girl. What do you know!"

Ronald Drake said, "Miss Hodson, Mr. Anders."

Craig Anders leaned toward her, balanced on both hands, so that his face was just above hers. His fingers were tanned and strong against the white tablecloth.

"You sly dog," Craig cried, "as they say in the British movies. Having a girl like this and never letting it out."

Ronald Drake was saying, "Craig is my roommate." He didn't sound happy about it.

Craig shook his head. "It would take a lovely creature like you," he said softly, "to get this guy out to a place like this."

Ronald said, "Nice to have seen you, Craig." He leaned forward and put one hand on Clara's arm. He tugged gently. "Baked Alaska?" he asked. "Or maybe baba au rhum?"

Clara swung her head slowly toward him, felt herself smiling dreamily and murmured, "Yes. Oh yes."

There was music all around them, soft and unlabored music. Craig said, "You don't mind if I steal her, do you? For just one dance?" He turned without a glance back at Ronald Drake. "Where did you come from, anyway?"

Clara's head went back again toward him. Her lips parted to let out a little sigh.

Ronald Drake said, "We're just about to have dessert—"

Clara found herself pulled to her feet. The brown hands were around her own, the dark eyes were close. She was vaguely aware of Ronald's solid glare, vaguely aware of a sense of guilt that he should be spending so much money on a girl who could be bewitched away from him like this. Then she didn't think any more because Craig Anders's arms were around her and his feet were moving in intricate patterns that took all of her concentration.

After a little his breath was blowing softly in her ear and his voice was whispering, "How did you ever let yourself get tied up with Ronnie-boy?"

"Mr. Drake is very nice," she said.

"Oh, nice." He pulled his face back away from her and she saw the underside of his chin. It was a charming chin, not as firm as Ronald Drake's. Like his arms. They were flexible around her and light, not sturdy.

"Ron's a good Joe," he went on. "Solid, dependable, house-in-the-suburbs-four-kids-and-a-raise-every-two-years guy." He shook his head and led her into a little off-beat twirl, and said, "Better things in life than that."

It sounded wonderful. It felt wonderful. It was the crowded room, all right. Except for her clear everyday mind. It asked, *what's wrong with a house in the suburbs? And kids?*

"But let's not talk about Ronnie-boy," Craig said. "Let's talk about you."

"Let's talk about you," Clara countered.

His smile was very sweet, very pleased. "All right," he agreed. "Let's."

"What about you?" she nudged.

The smile grew, the feet danced with joy. "I'm getting dizzier by the minute and at present between engagements as they say on the stage..."

And living with Ronald Drake for a little security, her everyday mind finished. *I hate myself,* Clara thought a little wildly. *Here it is, and here I am, and here he is, and how am I thinking?*

He pulled her suddenly closer, went into a spasm of short dipping swirls and Clara let herself go, tasting the moment, the wonderful combination of melody and rhythm.

When the music drifted to a close she opened her eyes. Craig's arm was still around her but it was suddenly an impersonal support. She followed his glance and saw that he was searching out the room, the way he had before. He was looking toward the head of the steps and everything about him was still.

The girl wore green, glistening satiny green, with no straps to cut the view of her magnificent creamy shoulders. Her hair was red and it flamed. She stood very still, tall and proud and sure of herself, and she searched the room, too, as if she were to meet somebody here. A muscle in Craig's cheek twitched and he made a movement toward the beautiful figure, then his arm became aware of its burden and he smiled down at Clara.

"Fine dance," he said. He took her arm and hurried her through the tables, back to her own. "Ronnie should have told me about you before."

The table was empty. A frown caught itself between his dark brows. "Wonder where old Ronnie got to," he muttered. He flipped one hand, turned and walked briskly away from Clara, toward the girl in green.

Well, that's that, Clara thought, watching the girl's exquisite face light up, her arms reach out, when she spied Craig. *That's it and what did you expect?* She felt weak, deflated. The table was pushed back on an angle, as if Ronnie had gotten up hurriedly, in anger perhaps. She looked at his plate. Under a soggy golden meringue, ice cream had melted and collapsed forlornly.

It told a story. Ronald had ordered the "outstanding dessert." He had seen it delivered, had sat there, watching Craig Anders whirl her about the floor, watching the ice cream melt. Ronald knew Craig, and the words that spilled out from his handsome mouth. In rage, or in disappointment, he had pushed back his chair and gone somewhere.

Clara tried to find him, among the tables, the dancers. It was hard to do. The tears in her eyes shared Ronald's disappointment with her. *It was the way Craig Anders came across the room to me*, she defended herself, *as if he had found me at last and was—impelled to. Don't you see?*

At the head of the stairs the red-headed girl was about to follow the headwaiter. All eyes were on her. Craig Anders was turned away from her. He was stepping back. He was reaching out to catch the gray sleeve of a man who tried to circle him. Ronald Drake! Clara found a deep sigh of relief going all through her. He was here. He hadn't just paid the check and left her.

Through the comforting thoughts, she watched Craig bend to whisper something to him. She saw his shrug, saw him reach in his pocket, pull out his wallet and inconspicuously tender a bill. She watched Craig pocket it, admiring his dexterity, the way his body shielded the exchange from the girl.

That was why, of course, her good clear efficient clerk-at-Helderson's mind told her. Craig needed that bill. He knew Ronald was coming to the Moon Roof. It was Ronald he looked for, there at the head of the stairs, whom he headed straight toward, winging his way. Not toward her, toward Clara Hodson, the pastel girl, whose dreams were silly and bright inside of her.

But Ronald had looked for her. He had said, "I've been watching you."

Well, she thought mournfully, *he'll never want to see me again. Not ever.* She should be feeling sad because Craig was following the girl now, down to one of the best tables. But instead, she saw the way she'd go up to Ronald and say, "I'd like to take my time out now." She saw the way he would turn his head so that he stared out over her and his nice voice would be cold and he would say, "Go. Go, by all means."

It made her feel awful. Her lips trembled and her hands shook and suddenly she knew that since the day Ronald Drake came to Helderson's, she had been watching him and thinking about him and it didn't matter what Marie said, he was no fuddy-duddy.

She straightened her shoulders. *It's exactly what you deserve,* she told herself scornfully. *You and your crowded room.*

She picked up her purse and looked toward the stairs. Ronald was stepping down them. Surely. Steadily. He was moving like an irresistible force. He was pushing his way through people, around them, between tables. He wasn't watching his feet, either. He had set his eyes on their destination.

He had set his eyes on her. With every step of the distance that he closed so decisively it seemed to Clara they grew bluer and brighter and more compelling. She watched him, fascinated and nervous, the drum beats of her heart making its previous confusion nothing but little watch ticks. Everything about Ronald grew larger than life size, until he was standing next to her.

It seemed like a long time before she could raise her eyes to look at him. She couldn't bear it if there was anger on his face, or scorn, or pity or disappointment.

None of those things was there. What she saw there took the breath completely away from her.

Ronald put out one commanding hand. Clara stood up. It was quite an effort, weak as she suddenly was. She put her own hand in his and felt immediately engulfed in warmth, the kind of warmth that was a house in the suburbs and four kids and a raise every two years. But which was more than that—was bubbles and sparkles and knowing.

He opened his mouth. Clara was lost in the tickle around her heart, the lack of breath, the certainty of what he would say.

He said it: "Let's get out of here!"

Ronald, she thought, allowing her fingers to press a little more tightly against the ones that held hers so closely, didn't have that chin for nothing. It didn't matter where they went from there, what adventures opened out to them, the tale had begun right, with a flare, with excitement, with promise.

"Yes, Ronald," Clara answered joyously.

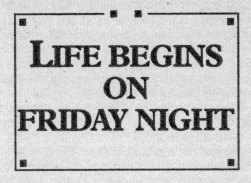

LIFE BEGINS ON FRIDAY NIGHT

When Joselyn picked up the receiver Beck said, "Honey, it's so miserable out. I'm holed up in this nice clean tourist cabin, and they serve hot dinners. I'm going over to get one, then take a shower and get to bed. Do you mind, dear?"

Joselyn's voice showed nothing of what she felt. She said, "Of course not, Beck. It's a foul night, and you must be dead, driving all the way from New York."

"I'll get up at daybreak," he promised. "I want to get home early. If this rain stops, Tom and I have a match."

"That will be nice." She studied the hand in her lap; the nails were long, oval and freshly painted, the palm scented with Beck's favorite cologne.

"How are the kids?"

"Wonderful as ever." She didn't mention the baby's cough. It had started on Monday. It was gone now—Friday night. Life begins on Friday night, she thought. Only not this Friday. Nor last Friday.

Beck said, "I certainly missed getting home last weekend."

"Was the deal successful?" she asked brightly. "No,

don't tell me about it now. I want to hear all the details."

Beck laughed. "What have you been doing?" he asked.

She waited a moment, smoothing out the silken legs of her lounging pajamas, thinking how long it had taken to press them to their present sleek look. Well, she could press them again in the morning and wear them tomorrow.

"This and that," she answered gaily. "Reading. The curtains—again. Teaching Serene to make that veal scallopini you liked at the Trainers'. Marcia drove over one day this week. We sat before the fire and drank tea and settled the world."

He laughed. "Sounds cozy."

"It was," she said. "Very." It's all cozy, she thought. Marcia and Anne and Doris in the daytime. The children. Books. Sometimes the radio. Five days a week. Five nights.

Beck yawned. It hummed over the wires, sounding close even through the the crackling of the rain against the windows.

"Poor dear," she sympathized, "I won't keep you. You've given me an idea. I'll get Ellen and Skip off to roost now. Then I'll take a shower myself and—"

"You really don't mind?" he asked. "I'm seventy miles away…"

"Which is much too far to come on a night like this. Of course I don't mind. Let's say good night now, dear. I'll see you in the morning, fresh and bright."

"Fresh and bright," he repeated. "'Night, beautiful." He hung up.

Suddenly Joselyn was angry, so angry that her short slim body couldn't hold it. She slammed the receiver down and raced into the kitchen.

Serene turned from the stove.

If ever, Joselyn thought through the blur of her

furious disappointment, a person was misnamed! Serene—the nervous wreck. Joselyn braced herself. "Serene," she began, keeping calm.

"I know, I know. I heard it. In bits, that is, and not meanin' to. And me fussin' and stewin' all day over this fancy dish that ain't goin' to warm up worth anything. You're too sweety-sweet to that man, ma'am, if you'll excuse me sayin' so. He walks on you—"

Joselyn kept her face expressionless, her eyes remote. "That's enough, Serene," she said quietly. "Mr. Ashley works very hard and travels all over the country. Sometimes he can get home—"

"And sometimes he can't. Yes, ma'am. I'll shut up." Serene smiled her sudden flash that was so out of keeping in the wrinkled tartness of her face. "Us women alone, way out here in the country, I get out of hand sometimes. You're too sweety-sweet to me, too, for a fact."

Joselyn reached for Serene's shoulder and gave it a quick pat. "I couldn't be," she vowed. "I'd go stark raving mad out here without you, and you know it."

She turned and ran upstairs, keeping her back straight, lifting her legs high. It was good exercise that way. She peeked into the nursery. Johnny was asleep on his stomach, with only the curve of his cheek, the stub of his nose and one curl visible.

"Bless you," she whispered and shut the door gently.

The anger returned, though, when she went into the playroom. Ellen and Skip were still sitting carefully on small chairs, books in their laps and the fresh clothes creased only in the necessary places. Her final words to them still hung in the air. "Be quiet and don't get mussed up. You want daddy to see you at your very best."

She swallowed. "Well, sugars," she cried, "we'll just take those Sunday-special things off and get into nice comfortable sleepers. And how would you like it if I brought your dinner up here and we had a party?"

She talked fast, but it wasn't good enough. Ellen's face folded from top to bottom like a rosy accordion, and her braids swung the way they always did when she was going to cry. Skip's mouth turned into a pink oval studded with white teeth, and a small wail started to emerge from it. Joselyn raced to him, put her hand gently over the gap and kissed his head. But not before the wail had reached its zenith, and Johnny waked from sleep to match it. Then Ellen screamed, "Daddy isn't coming home! Again. Again. He isn't coming home!"

It was almost nine o'clock by the time she managed to quiet them, feed them, read to them and bed them down. She walked slowly down the stairs, forgetting all about the importance of standing erect, slim and poised. In the living room she looked with distaste at the efforts of the week. The curtains were crisp, the many chrysanthemums fluffy, the cushions plumped up and waiting. But the fire was out; there wasn't even a puff of smoke rising from it.

She stood for a long moment in the dining room, staring blindly at the tall white candles she had driven all the way into the city to get. The linen matched their purity, and the silver gleamed.

Over the sink in the kitchen, on Serene's blackboard, she saw the note.

Went into town with Mrs. Harton's girl to see a movie. Got my key. Veal is in oven.

Serene

Joselyn turned off the warming oven and walked through the house snapping off light switches, locking doors. All the time her thoughts paced beside her, waiting for her to get to the secret point where the fear lay, to bring it out into the open and examine it.

Upstairs she sat before her dressing table and looked at her face, as she had a thousand times before. It was an odd face, thrown together helter-skelter, anchored only by the wide-set blue eyes. Everything else, she thought, was wrong: the nose too long, too thin, too pinched; the mouth too full. Her hair, banged slickly across the high, narrow forehead, hung in glossy smoothness below her ears, covering their largeness, thank heaven, completely.

I've done the best I could, she told herself. I've made the most of every asset. If that isn't enough, I don't know what I can do.

A little spurt of terror burned the back of her throat. The country was so full of pretty girls—really pretty ones—who didn't have to use rosy powder to cover sallow skin, who could pull their hair back carelessly with a bit of ribbon and look fresh and lovely. Offices, hotels, theaters, even tourist-camp restaurants, were full of pretty girls.

Joselyn's eyes stayed on her reflection, but she stopped seeing herself. She saw only her thoughts, almost as if they were screened before her. She recognized the element of gratitude in her love for Beck upon which she had built her life. Until he came, her mother and father's big house, the summer camps, the boarding school, the Junior League, the dramatic school, all had been a dull filling-in. Beck brought so much more that, somehow, she felt she never could do enough to repay him.

Joselyn had been rehearsing for the league play when Beck walked in that night long ago, with a thin, bespectacled boy who bore, with what grace he could, the name of Langley Badger. The two of them stood at the back of the hall watching as Joselyn, with her animated voice and her eager graceful movements, proved, or tried to prove, her belief that there were charms other than beauty.

When the director called a rest he said, smiling,

"Joselyn, I'm beginning to think you might really make an actress."

She sat down quietly, away from the casual, loud circle of the others in the cast. Those were the days when she studied everyone, adding their gestures, if good, to her own repertoire and carefully avoiding their mistakes. She could feel herself shaping up from them.

Then Langley Badger and a young man, who made Langley look too tall and too thin, came up to her. "This is Beck Ashley, Joselyn," Langley said. "He's come to Chicago to open a plant my father's putting money into." He swallowed his chagrin at having mentioned money and muttered, "Joselyn Mills... Beck."

She lifted her eyes to Beck's for the first time.

"You don't really want to be an actress, do you, Miss Mills?" he asked and smiled.

"Am I that bad?" she said. It sounded coy. All men's hair should grow the way his does, she thought.

He shook his head. "You're good," he said, "but I have other ideas."

Six months later he told her, "That first night, remember? I've often wondered how I happened to let Langley Badger take me anyplace, but I was so lonesome. That first night when I saw you up there, bright and gay, with that warm sweet voice—and so beautiful—I said to myself, 'There's the girl I'm going to marry.'"

From that moment on there was gratitude in her love. Beck didn't start her on the way to being the person she was to become. She had already decided that she always must be well-groomed, charming, interested in others. Personality, she had told herself, even as early as those bitter days in boarding school when it was the other girls who had the dates, could be far more important than looks.

But when Beck told her that he loved her she started a mental notebook. She noted in it all the things that pleased him. The first were: bright, gay, warm sweet voice, beautiful, beautiful, beautiful.

Now, staring into her mirror, Joselyn wondered where she had failed.

Beck once said about Marcia, "How Tom can stand her possessiveness I'll never know. Heaven deliver me from a woman who can't let her man out of her sight." That went into the notebook. When Beck wanted to play poker with the boys, or golf or chess, she kissed him goodbye lightly, greeted him gaily on his return. She never mentioned the empty hours she got through alone as best she could.

It wasn't that Beck demanded anything, really. He was such a happy, easy person. She felt comfortable with him—and secure, really secure in being a woman.

So in return for all this—this house, the way Beck looked at her just before he kissed her good-night, the way he said in front of friends, "Tell the story of the old lady you saw at the grocer's, Joselyn," and looked around proudly as she acted out the human little tale—for all this and much more, she had vowed to give him perfection.

Only this week she and Marcia had sat before the fire and talked about such things. Marcia was Joselyn's oldest friend and she spoke with privilege.

"I wish I didn't envy you," she'd said. "My house is a hodgepodge. My whole life seems a mess. I haven't any organization. Some days I wake up feeling like a mother and we have a picnic. Then other days I'm ugly as sin and screeching at everybody. Even with Louella in the kitchen I never seem to get anything shining and perfect, the way you do."

Joselyn had laughed. "Silly," she said, "nothing's perfect here. We're always in chaos. Except," she amended thoughtfully, "on weekends. Then things straighten out."

She'd thought of Marcia's house. Hodgepodge was

right—clothes piled on chairs, magazines scattered. Her two boys were rough, wild, handsome little animals who responded when they felt like it and were rude when they pleased.

Beck seemed proud of his three. "Where they get their manners is a mystery to me," he'd said once. "Not that we're boors, exactly, but most kids…" He let it go. But it warmed Joselyn. It repaid those weekdays when every other sentence from her lips seemed to be "Say please" or "Say thank you."

Marcia had taken a deep breath. "And I envy you your nice, polite marriage," she continued. "Tom and I…we've just quarreled. A nasty sort of quarrel, with screaming and words. But I can't imagine you and Beck like that. You're always so kind, so gentle with each other."

At that moment the fear touched Joselyn a little. Polite, yes. Gentle, yes. And kind. But Tom had to be pulled from his home by Beck's persuasion. And Beck—what went on in his mind? Why were there more and more times when he couldn't seem to get plane or train accommodations, and a weekend here, a weekend there went by without his coming home?

"Tom makes me so furious," Marcia went on, "he makes me cry. My face puffs up, and I look horrible when I cry. Then I'm madder than ever at him because he's made me look and act such a fool."

Beck, Joselyn thought proudly, has never seen me weep one tear. He has no idea what a crybaby I really am. He'd be utterly shocked if he saw me as Serene has, as my pillow has, when we have one of those days.

Marcia had risen from the deep chair. She stood for a time staring at her reflection in the big mirror over the stone mantel. Her short, curly black hair looked wild. Her lipstick was crooked. There was a hole in the elbow of her not-too-clean sweater, a series of impudent snags in her stockings. She'd sighed deeply. "Look at me, then look at you. Your dress is like lettuce, your hair's like silk and it curls under just where you want it. You never have a shiny nose or a split fingernail." She'd leaned toward Joselyn. "How do you stay that way?"

Joselyn laughed again and pushed aside the personal touch. "It's magic."

It's hard work, she thought. Marcia is really beautiful. She can afford to let herself go a little because the straightness of her profile, the curve of her lips, the lovely high line of her cheeks, is always there. But me... She smiled wryly, recalling the mornings she had made herself wake before Beck to hurry into the bath and brush her hair and put on her makeup.

But she didn't tell this to Marcia. The politeness, the perfection, the charm of always saying the right thing that was part of her life with Beck had become part of her life with everyone. She was extremely popular with old and young, rich and poor, and she knew why. She just submerged herself and focused her interest outward to make others feel important.

She did it again. She said earnestly, "Marcia, you're beautiful without even trying to be, and your home has that wonderful lived-in feeling. Why, your boys act as if you were one of them and could climb the highest tree in the world."

Almost visibly her words soaked into Marcia and colored her spirits again.

"Let's have some more tea," Joselyn had said, "then tell me what you think of the book I lent you."

Marcia had come over Tuesday. On Wednesday Joselyn ironed the curtains, on Thursday she waxed the floors. Now it was Friday night. It came back to that, and everything added together somehow.

Sitting before her dressing table, she creamed her face while she tried to put the pieces of her thoughts into some sort of pattern.

Let's be efficient about this, she thought. Beck no

longer seems eager to come home, no matter how
nicely he apologizes for his failure to arrive, no matter
how many reasons he has. When he does come he
plays golf with Tom all day Saturday. He wants to go
to the club on Saturday night. All day Sunday he
works in the yard when the weather's good, or down in
the basement when it rains. He expects to have friends
in on Sunday evening. Then it is Monday morning,
and he takes the early train or drives away before the
sun is fully out, and we haven't been together at all.
Not really. Not the way we once were.

Yet, in all honesty, when he does come home there is
everything waiting for him: an immaculate house, fine
food, happy children. There is—there is his wife—
scented and gay, sharing his anecdotes eagerly, never
bothering him with the muddiness of the driveway or
the times the car is stuck in the snow. Never telling
him about Skip's naughtiness or Ellen's tying the cat's
tail in a knot or the baby's colds. Never whining about
the boring, boring week and how much nicer it would
be to live in town where you could see somebody
besides the dry-cleaner, grocer, and laundry man. A
wife who chokes down the resentments that grow and
fester in loneliness and lets him see only the carefully
nourished, plucked, trimmed, flowering side.

She laughed aloud bitterly. "Saint Joselyn," she
scoffed. She dipped her fingers in a jar of rich yellow
lubricant and smoothed it thickly on her face, giving
special attention to the corners of her eyes. She cleaned
her hands and watched them impersonally as they
wound little sections of her hair into curls.

Joselyn stood up, peeled off the rumpled satin pajamas and shivered a moment, hearing the rain, angrier
than ever, against the house. Opening the chest in the
corner, she folded back the silks, satins and laces.
Down in one corner she found her white gown. She
pulled it out, held it up and murmured, "Good old
outing flannel, I love you."

She dropped it over her head. The soft warmth of it immediately hugged her and took away the shivers. From the back of the closet, behind the feathered mules and the trim, high-heeled shoes, she dragged a pair of sheepskin-lined slippers. Her toes wriggled happily in their depths.

She didn't look in the mirror this time. She knew what she would see. This outfit was her favorite one, except for the weekday dungarees and the sensible flat-heeled shoes.

She looked over the books on the bed table. They were all new, all erudite, all inestimably dull. "Not tonight," she said aloud. She shuffled out of the room, down the stairs and through the hall to Serene's room. Serene had quite a collection of love and detective stories. Joselyn chose a few and went into the kitchen.

There she worked efficiently, slicing dark rye bread, Bermuda onions, sharp cheese. She made two sandwiches, took a bottle of beer from the refrigerator and carried her loot into the living room. She piled pillows on the sofa and settled herself luxuriously.

The sandwich was stinging and refreshing in her mouth. The onion burned comfortably in her stomach and the tangy beer put out the little flame. The stories were gory, exciting, highly unliterary and very relaxing.

After a while she heard Serene's key in the lock.

"You still up, Mrs. Ashley?" Serene called. "I won't come in. My shoes is squashin'."

"How was the movie?"

Serene replied with an endless resume of the plot, and Joselyn listened sleepily. When the monologue stopped she called, "Good night," and heard Serene's door close.

She lay there, staring at the ceiling. So many women seem to feel their husbands are their just due, she thought, or even that they deserve something better.

Beck, she prayed, please, please don't get tired of me. I
try so hard.

She fell asleep. Sometime later she woke with a jump
that sent her heart racing. The tapping sound that had
roused her came again. Her throat closed with a terrible fear. She couldn't move, she couldn't breathe. As
she turned her eyes in the direction from which the
sound had come, a shadow blocked itself against the
windowpane—a shadow with a turned-down hat brim
and a square silhouette of powerful male shoulders.

Joselyn's mind took in, all in a moment, the long
muddy driveway to the street; the trees that shut the
house from view; the nearest neighbor a quarter of a
mile distant; the telephone 30 feet away in the hall;
Serene, nervous, excitable, no good in a crisis; the
children sleeping upstairs. Her thoughts raced for
some solution, some strength to get her from this
spotlighted sofa into a dark, defensive position.

She tried swinging one leg to the floor. Amazingly it
obeyed her command. She followed it with the other
and sat up. She deliberately ignored the window,
forced herself to yawn and tried not to jump when the
tapping grew louder and vague echoes of a rumbling
voice came to her above the wind and rain. She walked
carefully across the room to the hall.

The tapping turned to pounding on the door, solid,
furious pounding that demanded entrance. She re-
mained motionless, waiting to faint from shock. Then,
in a cessation of wind, she heard the voice.

"Joselyn," it cried, "let me in! For heaven's sake,
it's Beck, Joselyn!"

Without thinking, she reached for the light switch
and clicked it with trembling fingers. Relief was like
an ache as she started for the door.

Then on the heels of the first terror there came
another, different but just as gripping and twice as
strong. She looked down at her flannel gown. She saw

herself, pitiful, defenseless, exposed in the hall light.
Her mind sent her madly upstairs to fix her face, comb
her hair, change into the seductive pajamas. But her
feet stayed rooted. How long had he been there at the
window watching her? It didn't matter. He could see
her clearly now. The jig, she thought, walking steadily
to the door, is up. But up, my girl.

She turned the lock, swung the door wide and stepped
back to admit the soaked figure of her husband.

He came in, closing the door slowly behind him, not
taking his eyes from her face. "Changed my mind," he
explained. "Forgot my key." Rain dripped from the
brim of his hat to his shoulders to the floor.

"You're making puddles," she said foolishly.

He nodded. There was a look in his eyes Joselyn had
never seen before. There was a little twitching at one
corner of his mouth she never wanted to see again.

Suddenly, watching him mechanically taking off his
hat and topcoat, his eyes never leaving her face, she
flared in fury. "How sure can you be?" she cried, not
at all sweetly or warmly. "Seventy miles away, you
said, and a miserable night! And you'd rather not come
home anyway. All right, so you did, and the nerve of
you! You have no right to surprise me. I hate surprises.
I hate being alone and waiting for you week after week.
And being disappointed at the last minute. And having
Ellen get sick because you said you'd come and you
didn't. And staying out here in this forsaken place
with nobody to talk to. And afraid to let go and be
myself with anybody—anybody at all anymore—
because I love you so much and I'm so afraid you'll
find somebody who's really wonderful and doesn't
have to work at it. And you've no right—"

She wasn't making sense. She wanted to stop and
she couldn't. She cried, "Make me stop this screaming, Beck. Make me! I don't want to scream. I don't
want to cry." Hiccups shook her, and tears rolled

down her cheeks over the lubricating cream.

Then she felt Beck's coat against her flannel gown and his arms under her knees. She put her greasy face against his shoulder. He carried her into the living room and sat down with her. He rocked her back and forth, not saying a word. After a while her sobs lessened.

Beck spoke at last. "Quite a batch of reading matter you have here," he said calmly.

She didn't look at him.

"I recognized the beer, of course," he went on, "but I didn't know what kind of a sandwich it was until you started blowing in my face."

"All right," she said fiercely, "so now you know. I like comfortable old clothes and onion sandwiches. I simply adore blue cheese. Your kids are little demons and they drive me crazy five days a week. I get tired of improving my mind so I'll have something to talk with you about. I get tired of being well-groomed and ladylike and uncomplaining."

She sat up straight, but Beck's strong arms pulled her back against him.

"You certainly do," he said mildly. "It's what's known as a pendulum swing, isn't it?"

"And you," she went on, more quietly but with distilled anger and sorrow, "you get the cream of it all every weekend—every weekend that you're interested enough to come home and skim it, that is. You're as free as the breeze, as welcome as springtime and as handsome as a collar ad. And I think I hate you."

Beck started with Joselyn's curls. He scanned her forehead, her nose, her mouth, her ears. He appraised the nightgown and examined the slippers. Joselyn felt the red of pure unhappiness flooding her face. The ache within her was beyond tears now.

When Beck's eyes came back to hers there was warmth in them. His mouth curled wide and he began to laugh. The sound of it seemed to fill the whole room.

Joselyn tried not to share it. She tried very hard to keep the fury on her face, but she could feel it sliding away; the tickle of merriment began to grow in her, too, and she joined him. Once more the tears, haphazard and ridiculous, slid over the cream.

Beck pulled her close to him. Between chuckles he said, "Hate me, do you? Well, I don't believe a word of it. But you almost had me fooled. What an effort you've made. It was beginning to bore me stiff."

She pulled away, trying not to give him the benefit of onion. "Bore you?" she asked incredulously.

He nodded, serious at last. "You've been pretty hard to live up to, honey," he explained. "Think I could swear in this house? Or lose my temper? Or sing a rowdy song? Or talk about anything that really bothered me?" He shook his head. "Not a chance. This was a little piece of heaven and, by heaven, you had to live up to it. Only a lug would disturb the peace. Sometimes, after a bad week, I just couldn't make the effort to try."

Joselyn drew a deep, deep breath. Her whole body felt light with relief and her mind was filled with the beautiful knowledge of security—a security far more wonderful than any she had known before.

"Josie," Beck whispered. "Josie." It was as if the silly, tender little nickname had been in the back of his mind always, waiting for a moment like this. He lowered his face toward hers.

"Onions," Joselyn whispered back.

He shook his head impatiently. "I'll eat some myself in a moment. That'll fix it."

His lips came down eagerly against hers. It was a kiss like no other kiss. It skidded a little on the lubricating cream, but it knew what it was about and righted itself almost at once.

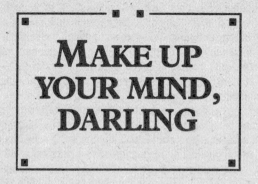

MAKE UP
YOUR MIND,
DARLING

Mrs. Humphrey's fist was power on the door. Her voice was power right through it. "Rise and shine, Johnny," she called, as she did every morning, even this morning when she knew he'd be up.

He stood on the other side of the door, his blue pajama bottoms wrinkled from his night's restlessness, the brown of his thin chest and arms sharp contrast.

"Up and at it," he called back.

"Your best white shirt is hanging in your closet," Mrs. Humphrey yelled. "And I bought you a new pair of socks."

"Why, bless your little pointed head," Johnny cried, and went to look.

Nobody could iron a shirt like Mrs. Humphrey, he thought, looking at the starched perfection hanging beside the new dark blue suit. He touched it with a tentative finger. Could Marilee iron at all? Could she even cook?

It didn't seem to matter. He went to the mirror, lifted his chin, pushed out his chest and pulled in his nonexistent stomach. He leaned close to the glass, so that his breath made a fog for him to leer through.

What did she see in him, that girl of delight, that laughing elf? It was such a serious dark face, long and narrow and with too-thick eyebrows.

He shrugged and walked over to the dresser. The new socks lay there, the price tag still pinned inside. Ninety-eight cents, and Mrs. Humphrey couldn't afford it. *Call it a wedding present,* he thought, *and it's okay. Everything's okay.*

Suddenly, with his hand on the socks, the "okay" became little licking flames of fear in the back of his head. He began to shake and he couldn't seem to stop. Johnny Brandon's wedding day. Marriage. Marital bliss. The institution of matrimony. A noose around the neck. Hank Winters's voice saying, "Poor boy. Poor kid. You don't know when you're well-off."

He shook his head abruptly, yanked off the pajamas, pulled on old shorts and dungarees and a T-shirt, slipped his feet into sneakers and went into the big, old-fashioned bathroom. He brushed his teeth, not looking himself in the eye, and put some goo on his hair, hoping it would do the trick in three hours. Three hours.

The panic rose again. He pushed it firmly back and walked toward the stairs. He glanced in his room. The pajama bottoms were a blue puddle on the waxed floor. He went in and picked them up, folded them carefully and tucked them into the bottom dresser drawer. Might as well start good habits now. Mrs. Humphrey didn't mind, but you couldn't tell about Marilee.

He swallowed the hot coffee too fast, letting it burn, just as he let Mrs. Humphrey rattle talk around him.

"Be sure and be on time," Mrs. Humphrey was commanding. "You know how you are, Johnny. You get off at the garage or down at the hardware store or on the golf course and time just gets the best of you."

She slapped four hotcakes down on his plate, added

two eggs, their yolks ogling sunnily at him, and pushed the syrup bottle nearer. Then she stood, hands on hips, and beamed down at him.

"Lord knows I'm going to miss you, Johnny," she said. "Like my own son, I always say. Six years isn't sneezing time."

Six years, Johnny thought. He tried to smile back at her. He reached for a fork and tried to spread butter on the cakes. He failed in both missions. "I'm going to miss you, too," he admitted rustily.

Bunder, the old scottie, padded over to him and nuzzled his leg. Tears popped into Mrs. Humphrey's outstanding blue eyes, and Johnny wanted to call the whole thing off.

He got up abruptly, knocked over his empty cup, stepped on a yelping Bunder and bumped Mrs. Humphrey's more-than-adequate shoulder. "Gotta lot to do," he muttered. "Can't eat anymore now."

He knew without looking that her chins trembled. They always trembled at the sacrilege of somebody refusing food. Any food, but especially hers.

Outside, Johnny stood on the porch and watched the sunshine try to infiltrate the knotted roots of the wisteria roof. He put his hands in his pockets and sniffed the vine's fragrance. Six years ago it had smelled this way when he walked up the porch steps. The only steps he'd seen that looked like those were the ones back at the orphanage. Satiny smooth, worn to a hammock in the middle by a million feet.

Six years ago he had noticed the steps, smelled the wisteria, rung the doorbell and faced Mrs. Humphrey.

"I'm Johnny Brandon," he had said, and she had known him at once, as he knew her. Because of Flaps, because of her boy, because Flaps had told Johnny about her those long quiet hours before the hot brazen one in which he had been killed, and because Flaps had written her about Johnny.

Flap's picture was on the piano. Johnny dumped his barracks bag in the wide hall and tried not to look at it.

"Eat first and then tell me," Mrs. Humphrey ordered. She marched him to the kitchen and he ate that time, and right. He ate as if he had never tasted food before—and, in a way, he hadn't. Not Mrs. Humphrey's. Not served with her joy.

Now he walked down the steps and across the lawn that he had mowed last Saturday. He wondered with a sort of awe how it had all happened. How that barracks bag had been unpacked and the things put away in the old dresser of the upstairs front room. He wondered how Old Man Hunnigan had said yes so readily to his asking for a job at the garage, and he wondered where all the years were before he came to High Hill and Mrs. Humphrey.

The sun hit his shoulder blades. Yesterday he and Marilee had gone to the beach. The sun had touched them in just that way, only more insistently. It burned a little on the corners of his shoulders as it always did. Marilee had put her hand on one of them.

"Bony," she had said. "So long and bony. You have good bones, though. Pop says bones show breeding."

Breeding, Johnny had thought, and pulled his shoulder away. He rolled over onto his stomach. The words that he should say, that he had tried to say a thousand times since he met her, were written in his mind. "Our kids," he should say, "will be sure of only part of their heritage. Me, Marilee, I'm an orphan. I don't know a single darned thing about my folks. Only the Home and finally being old enough to get out, to go to war and then High Hill." What would she say then? Her father and mother, what would they say?

"You have no family?" Mrs. Martin had asked the first time he went to the big house to call for Marilee.

There had been only kindness in her voice, but he had said, "No family," and left it there. It was true, wasn't it?

Later, when he saw how it was going to be with him and Marilee, he tried to tell her. But you don't take chances with a girl like Marilee Martin. You don't do anything to cut your own throat or cheapen your own stock.

It was bad enough that he worked in Old Man Hunnigan's garage, even if he had almost saved the amount to buy a partnership. A garage is a long way from a typewriter, from the city people who came for weekends.

When the Martins came to town, Mrs. Humphrey said, "Isn't it something to have a celebrity like Simpson Martin in High Hill? And him just as nice and friendly…"

And he was, too, acting as if Johnny Brandon had a right in the big white house with the pillars, was welcome in the swimming pool and at the table. But you can't tell with a man like Simpson Martin, either. They have manners, people like him, which cover a lot of feelings.

Johnny went to the garage as he knew he would. Old Man Hunnigan was under the jalopy that belonged to Hank Winters. The car was so old and crotchety that it spent more time in the garage than out. Johnny kicked his sneaker against the old man's turned-up flat feet. There was rustling, rumbling, muttering, then the Old Man emerged.

He wasn't very old, for a fact, but the grease of his livelihood was etched deep in the lines of his face, and his hair was grayish black, the exact shade of worn-out oil.

"What you doin' here, boy?" he cried. "Git on home and git your rest. Dig some of the dirt out of your nails. Girls is fussy about such things, girls brought up fancy and fine like yours."

Johnny looked surreptitiously at his hands. There was a rim of black caught beneath each nail. "I tried," he said. "Want me to give the jalopy a look?"

It seemed terribly important to get down under the car, to hold a wrench or a screwdriver in his hands.

"You off your rocker?" Old Man Hunnigan scoffed. "Try turpentine. Wife's got a soap, makes it herself. Go ask her."

He gave Johnny a push and the young man found himself turned around and shuffling slowly out of the kind dimness into the hot street again. He knew a quick anger at the old man. He felt rejected, somehow, like those times at the Home when people would come and look them all over and take somebody else.

He paced past the fairgrounds and up the curling, hilly road to the golf course. It wasn't much of a course, but it lay high and low and in between, and Johnny loved every inch of it.

He stood beside the caddie house and looked up to the first tee. There, right there, early one Sunday morning, he had seen Marilee for the first time.

"That's the Martin girl," Hank had said. They stood quietly together and Johnny knew that Hank was watching the way the wind blew her skirt back, her hair back, just as he was. But when she gripped the club, when it pulled back with beautiful rhythm and swung forward with precision, their heads swung with it to watch the small ball that lifted through the air and soared clean and true for two hundred yards.

Johnny found himself walking away from Hank quickly, as if Hank might follow. He moved up to the girl.

"That was a beautiful drive," he offered. "I'm playing alone. Are you?"

She smiled at him, her first smile, the polite one, but even that was enough to wrinkle something inside Johnny that had never been touched before. "Not any more," she said. She stood aside and gestured. "Your turn, sir."

She was four strokes ahead by the third green, and he knew her name was Marilee. She'd be glad to have breakfast with him; she called him Johnny; this was the first public course she'd played on but she loved it. *Look all around you at the fresh morning, Johnny. See how still and sleepy the town looks? Will we do this every Sunday morning, Johnny?*

We will, we did. The diner always seemed steamy and enclosed when they sat down for breakfast. She ate as she played golf, like a man, but there the resemblance stopped. Her hands were small and firm the time she showed him a putting grip, and he knew then how it would be.

It was the fourth Sunday, in the rough beside the two big elm trees, that it happened. It was the first time he had kissed a girl who was in the middle of a laugh, a girl who kissed him back so that his breath stopped and he thought he would never get it again, and then, when the kiss was over, finished the laugh as if it was too important to leave dangling.

He stood now beside the elm tree and he felt it again. Was she pretty, Marilee? He had never stopped to wonder, really. She had eyes that were no color and every color and eyebrows that tilted up at the outside corners. She had very short blond hair that seemed to move, to be blowing always with the vitality, the happiness that filled her slim body, her voice, her smile.

"That was good," she had said with a laugh when the kiss was done. "That was just about the finest kiss I've ever had, Johnny Brandon."

You laughed at something like that, didn't you? Even if you were dead serious, with a ripple all through you like your blood vessels were trembling. "Me, too," he said, and they shouldered their bags and finished the game.

Johnny touched the bark of the tree trunk. "Marilee," he whispered, and felt foolish.

He went back to the caddie house and collected a bucket of balls and an iron. He stood on the driving range, slamming out the balls until they were all gone. Slamming hard, as if he was hitting something he hated, trying to get even with somebody.

He looked at his watch and one hour was gone.

Back in town, Hank Winters was leaning against the hardware-store window, working systematically at his teeth with a fresh broom straw. He kept a broom in a corner of the glassed-in cubicle he called his office just for that purpose.

Johnny leaned beside him. "Hi," he said.

Hank sniffed. "Hi, yourself. Why aren't you home?" He wiggled his shoulders. Hank always wiggled his shoulders. He had piloted a B-29 and his father-in-law's hardware store drove him crazy. "You getting a last taste of freedom?"

Johnny thought it over. "I guess I am," he admitted at last.

"Savor it while you may," Hank went on. "They'll hog-tie you and cut you down to size, and nothing you do from now on will be right. Especially a dame like Marilee, out of your class. You're not right in the first place. Mark my word. You're a dead duck."

There was a rim of bitterness in his voice. Everybody in town knew that Hank's wife held the whip hand. Felt sort of sorry for her, though, the way Hank was out every night after supper hunting up a poker game.

Hank said abruptly, "Pay me no mind, kid. I'm sour. I had it, up there in the air. I had it in my hands and my heart and I'll never have it again. Isn't her fault. Isn't anybody's fault—not even the nuts' and bolts' and lawn mowers'." He swung sharply away from Johnny and disappeared through the slapping screen door.

Johnny sighed. He felt tired suddenly, and it was more than the sleepless hours of last night. He felt as if he was waiting for something terrible to happen.

What's so terrible about getting married, he asked himself. Getting married to Marilee. It sounded like a song title. *When I marry Marilee, that will be the end of me....*

"You're a very quiet man, aren't you?" Marilee had said once. They sat, feet dangling, at the edge of the pool, and all around them laughter swirled. Sometimes Johnny thought there was too much laughter at the big house. Everybody very gay, not knowing a thing about orphanages and war and people like Mrs. Humphrey who carried courage in every ounce of her considerable weight. Everybody laughing and forgetting you had to make a living, saying, "Where you off to, Johnny?" Pulling up to the garage and saying, "Whaddya know, Marilee's somber man."

That wasn't fair. Only one of them said that. Only the very blond, very tweedy one from the city. Vance Lane. He was too handsome. He was also very much in evidence around Marilee.

"God's angry man," he repeated. "Marilee's somber man. Out of your league, aren't you, buddy?"

One of the drives from the range had been for Vance Lane, this day.

The trouble was, Vance and Marilee looked so right together. They moved the same way, with assurance and abundant good health and teeth straightened and vitamins. After Vance's remark, Johnny stayed away from Marilee.

Five days later, she came into the garage. She kicked his foot as he had this morning jounced the old man's. "Get out from under there," she said. "You cowardly, hiding bum. Explain yourself."

He didn't want to, but he came out. He wasn't even fully straightened before she had her arms around him and was laughing against his cheek and pulling his hair and getting grease all over herself. It began to dawn on him then, the miracle that was so hard to believe.

That night on the beach, sitting before the fire and watching the hot dogs turn brown on their sticks, he tried to say it to her.

"Marilee," he said, swallowing hard, wishing he had Mrs. Humphrey's easy way with words, "it's been a lot of fun—the golf and breakfasts, and even the parties at your house—"

She put her head on his shoulder and looked straight up at the sky. "Spangled," she said.

"But," he went on slowly, "it's too rich for my blood."

There was a tiny silence. Johnny heard his heart thud through it.

"You're dog's done to a crisp," Marilee cried suddenly. She jumped up and rescued the dangling stick. She slapped a bun around the black frankfurter and she jabbed it toward him. "Eat," she cried. "That'll learn you."

He took a forced bite. The skin was sour in his mouth.

"Oh, pooh," she said. "You can have mine." She came back and sat beside him. After a while she put his arm around her. She smiled up at him. He kissed her. That was that.

Johnny looked at his watch and quickened his steps. He had only an hour and a half left. Left? Zero hour, he thought, and it didn't seem funny.

"You're a very serious Joe," Marilee had said another time. "When you smile it's like the sun comes out, but there's too much thunder to suit me."

"Vance Lane is sunny enough," Johnny found himself saying.

"Aha!" Her eyes sparkled. "Jealous. Goody, goody."

"Jealous?" he repeated lightly, as if the word was to be scorned. *Jealous*, he thought underneath. *If you could know how it eats and eats...*

Marilee said, "Don't you think it's time we told my folks—before they begin to get some wild ideas about

Vance, too?"

He stood still and dropped her hand. He searched her face. It was clear and happy, the way it always was. As if she meant what she said.

"Tell them what?" he managed to ask.

"About us. About when we're going to be married."

His heart and his feet stopped at the same time. "Married?" He mouthed the word as if it were in a foreign language.

She grinned at him. "I know, I know," she cried. "Mrs. Humphrey takes care of your creature comforts in a wonderful way. Those pies, those cakes, those pressed suits. But there's more to it than that, brother. There's the snug security of your own little home—"

"What home?" he asked.

"The three-room apartment in the old Blaisdell place," she answered promptly. "Only I meant to save that for a surprise. I can't seem to keep anything from you."

"Can't you, Marilee?" he asked soberly.

Her smile didn't waver. "Nope," she said. "So how about seeing my folks—just for the old-fashioned, make-them-happy, only-child-asks-permission sort of deal?"

Sometimes when you get a balloon—they used to get balloons at the Home at Christmas—you blow and blow and you can't get it started. Then, just when you think it will never grow, never turn big and bright, it lets go and rounds itself. It gets so large it seems as if it might pull you right off the earth itself by its very size and lightness.

That's the way it was with Johnny then. As if a balloon grew in his chest, pushing out everything but happiness. So he didn't mind the walk up the hill to the big house, didn't worry as he stood beside Marilee and looked into the faces of her parents, the unsurprised faces.

All he did was hold Marilee's hand and grin foolishly, clutch Mr. Martin's welcoming grip and let

Mrs. Martin kiss his cheek. He just rode along with that balloon then, and the days since then, as light and free and happy as a lark.

Until this morning. Until that pair of socks. Since then the air had been sizzling out of the balloon, and he felt as if it were spiraling very slowly inside him, getting smaller and smaller with the old man's words, with Hank's face, with the remembrance of Vance Lane's rightness and the Home and Mrs. Humphrey's watering eyes.

He walked across the porch of the house. He thought, *I'm safe with Mrs. Humphrey. She knows about me and she lets me be myself. It's different from being my mother, and better, almost, because she makes up for so much. You have to laugh with Marilee. How long will her laugh last, there in a three-room apartment, with just my salary and eventually learning about me?*

He thought, *I have to tell her now. Tell her it's no go. I'm just Johnny Brandon and I belong in a comfortable old rooming house. I belong with Old Man Hunnigan and Mrs. Humphrey and Hank. Marilee is bright and gay and full of whims her parents indulge—and I'm one of them. It doesn't matter if the wedding is all set. I can't let her get into it. Not with me, Johnny "No-Name Garage" Brandon.*

He opened the squeaking door and walked to the phone. He lifted the receiver and heard Mrs. Humphrey's voice behind him from the kitchen. He put it down.

"That's him now," she was saying. "Quiet as a mouse, but I always hear him. I was the same way with Flaps. Johnny tell you about Flaps?"

No, I didn't, he answered silently. *I never told anybody about Flaps.*

"No, he didn't," a voice answered, and it was Marilee's. She had no right to be here one hour before the wedding. "He hasn't told me much of anything. I've had to guess for myself."

Johnny moved, impelled, toward the kitchen and the voices. His sneakers made no sound. He meant them not to this time.

"That's why I'm here," Marilee said. Her voice sounded defiant.

"And you most certainly shouldn't be," Mrs. Humphrey said, as if she was attacking an argument again. "It's bad luck for a bride to let herself be seen before the ceremony." She tried to lower her voice. "Be a good girl now and sneak out the back way before he comes out here. Go on, now."

Marilee was stubborn. "I have to see Johnny," she said. The kitchen door swung open with force. It knocked against Johnny's shoulder and threw him off-balance. He sat down abruptly on the floor.

Marilee leaned over him. "I'm sorry," she said formally. "Did I hurt you and what were you eavesdropping for?"

Johnny lied, rubbing his arm, "No and I wasn't eavesdropping."

Marilee sat down beside him on the dining-room floor. She ran her finger around the design of a faded cabbage rose in the rug.

Johnny said, "I expect you're here because you've come to the same conclusion I have."

She said nothing. Her breath was little and ragged in the silence. *Mrs. Humphrey must be listening with held breath herself,* Johnny thought.

"I was just going to call you," he said. "I wanted to talk to you."

"I want to talk to you, too," Marilee answered.

There was something strange. Her voice sounded as little as her breath. Only natural, of course. It's not easy to jilt a man an hour before the wedding.

"I want you to know that I wish you the best in the world," Johnny said hardly. "That's not me."

She shook her head numbly.

Johnny nodded. "I've done a lot of thinking this morning, walking all over town..."

"I was afraid of that," Marilee said in a whisper.

Johnny knew what was wrong when she turned her head and looked directly at him. What was wrong was that there was no laughter in her voice, in her eyes, on her lips.

"I've done a lot of thinking, too," she said somberly.

Johnny's heart sat like sudden ptomaine in the pit of his stomach. All right, so he'd worked himself up to the idea that it was a mistake, that he wasn't good enough for her. But he knew, sickly, that he didn't want to be agreed with. That he wanted somebody, specifically Marilee, to deny it fiercely, wildly, to persuade him that he should hurry upstairs, get all duded up and race to the big house to stand there, trembling and white, while she walked in beauty to him. That was what he needed. Needed badly, too.

Instead there was this quiet, serious girl he had never met before, who was about to tell him that she didn't really love him, that she hoped they would always be friends....

"I can't ever be friends with you," he said loudly from his thoughts. "And I'm not going to pretend—"

She didn't seem to hear him. "I couldn't sleep last night," she said. She pushed back her hair from her forehead. It was a weary gesture and it made Johnny want to cry. "I lay awake all night, thinking."

"So did I," he said.

"I thought about the first day and how I let you pick me up, and the first kiss, and following you to the garage that time—"

She stared down at her hands, knotted on her skirt. It was a denim skirt, one she wore for golf. No white satin. Not today, thank you.

I can't live without this girl, Johnny thought suddenly. *I don't care if I'm sprung from apes and haven't a dime and eat with a knife—I can't live without this*

*girl. Let her put on that fancy dress, please. Let her
come to the three-room apartment. Let her want to try
it. Give me a chance to show her, to make her want to
stay....*

He saw her mouth move again and tore himself away
from his frantic prayers. "And then...I really proposed
to you, you know. I dragged you to the folks and...and
sort of compromised you. I found us the apartment.
How I didn't realize before—" She put one hand over
her mouth, then moved it decisively away. "Why,
Johnny Brandon," she said at last, "I threw myself at
you every single minute from that day on the first tee.
And you never so much as said you loved me.
You never were more than a...than a...fellow traveler!"

He watched the sudden trembling of that mouth
made for laughter, the way the tears spurted from her
eyes, and he reached. He reached hard and fast and
held tight.

"Love you?" he heard from a distance in a voice that
had to be his. "Love you? I love you. Hear it? Love
you. Every way and forever and I'm an orphan and I
haven't anything, not even a name—"

"Orphan," she muttered, muffled by him. "I know
that."

Kissing away a laugh was good, but kissing away
tears was much better. Oh, much.

"Orphan," Mrs. Humphrey boomed above them in
repetition. "You think that's a secret? You think I ever
kept a secret? Everybody knows it. Always has. Besides, it isn't properly true. You got a family. You got
me."

Johnny tightened his hold on Marilee, but he looked
up at Mrs. Humphrey. "That I have," he said.

"Whim-whams, flim-flams, the vapors, last-minute
cold feet, whatever you call it, you two got the worst
case I ever seen." She reached her bulk forward. She
stretched for Johnny's hand, she stretched for Marilee's. "Come on, you kids. That wedding music is

going to have to go round and round filling in time if you don't step on it.''

They were on their feet, unsteady and sheepish.

It started inside Mrs. Humphrey this time, a bubble of laughter that churned a little before it reached her lips. It bumped against Marilee's and bounced around the room. It was joined at last, a little reluctantly, by a hearty masculine boom that swung both their heads toward Johnny.

"Whaddya know?" Mrs. Humphrey gasped. "He laughs best.''

"I laugh last," Johnny said. He tilted Marilee's face toward his. "I love you," he repeated.

She nodded. She looked as if she believed him, would believe him forever. As he believed himself.

He turned her around, his hand lingering on her shoulder. She felt known to him, familiar, shared somehow, as she never had before. "Scoot," he said.

Without a backward look, finished now with backward looks, he raced up the stairs to his room. He picked up the socks and stared at them for a moment. Then he went into the bathroom and turned the water on, hard and full, and started to shave. His watch said that he had exactly 37 minutes of freedom before the ax would descend.

He grinned at the lathered face reflected in the mirror. Fat chance any ax had to cut against the big, solid, floating, permanent balloon of Johnny Brandon's joy.

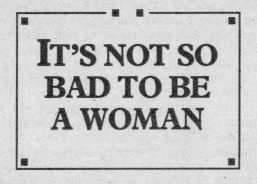

IT'S NOT SO BAD TO BE A WOMAN

Let me tell it my way, for once. When you're standing "where the brook and river meet," your reluctant feet get stalled by older people. This is my story. Nobody has a right to say, "Edey, not so loud," or "Edey, don't be such a tomboy."

This is my story. It's about me and Dud and Uncle Paul and my mother. It's about daddy, too, in a way, although he died when I was ten. I'm almost fifteen now, but I remember.

I remember he always took me fishing. When my mother would say, "Dave, she's not a boy and there's no use making her into one," daddy would snort. His snorts started in his throat. Silly and cheerful and scornful all at once. "It's a lot more sensible for her to learn to do the thing a man enjoys than to be pretty and ruffly and useless, Dora."

Mother's lip trembled. Mother was pretty and ruffly.

After daddy died, my mother tried to make a little lady out of me. There were two girls down the street. They had long yellow curls and wore pink dresses with lace on them. Dud and I never even asked them to join our gang. They couldn't climb a tree on a double dare. They squealed and hid where you could find them easy when we played Run, Sheep, Run. My mother thought they were wonderful. She put my hair up in curlers. It was all out by noon. I got a terrible ribbing at recess. But that was a long time ago, of course. The time I'm telling about is almost practically right now.

Yesterday morning I woke up quickly, the way I always do. When I stretched my feet toward the bottom of the bed, the muscles in the calves of my legs knotted and ached. I wiggled my toes. The knots smoothed out a little. I lay still and thought about the day before. It looked dim and long. Roller skating. Baseball in Henderson's lot. Fishing. All that was left of yesterday was the ache in my long thin legs. I could hear my mother's voice, "Like a colt's exactly."

Funny. One minute I was asleep, wrapped in a black-velvet secret place. Like my poetry in my five-year diary, which nobody knows about, not even Dud. Then something tore the black velvet, and there I was. Awake, with the feeling going through me. It was good, like a warm glow. It was a feeling I've had ever since I got to be fourteen. "Something wonderful will happen today." Every morning those words went through my mind.

I ran to the window. My loose pajamas pushed softly against my hard stomach. I watched the sun slide under and around the shade. Like melted butter. I grabbed the string-covered ring and gave it a tug. The shade clattered to the roller. It talked itself quiet. I looked at the day, framed in white ruffled curtains.

When I was alone everything was clear and exciting. The canna bed in Dud's backyard. The bushes that had a path worn through them, a little brown river through mountains. Dud's bicycle with the blue scratched off where he ran into the tree, trying to go no hands. The trellis up over the porch roof, which we painted last summer. When I was alone I saw it all. The poetry seemed to be in all of it. Without any words.

I watched Dud's window with the shade down tight. Dud never woke up fast the way I did. On summer days with the windows open, you could hear his mother trying to get him up. She started down low, like my singing lessons. Every time she called, "Dud get up!" she went higher. Finally she sounded like Lily Pons, only not so sweet.

I turned a cartwheel, jumped over the hallway and landed beside my mother.

"Edey!" she cried. "Please!"

Poor mother. She's been saying "please" at me ever since I can remember.

Mother looked nice, ready to go to work. Her seersucker suit was fresh and clean. She had a big hat on her red curls that made her face round and pink and soft. She smelled like lily of the valley. Sissy, but nice. She picked up her big bag that matched her hat and put her arm around my shoulder. I kind of held stiff and quiet. I don't know why. I always did.

She sighed. "You're so much like your father," she said.

"Am I?" I headed for my room. "I'm glad."

She sighed again. "Hurry into your clothes and come have coffee with me, honey," she said.

I pulled on my overalls and saddle shoes and gave my teeth a quick brush. Mother was at the table when I got downstairs. Liza had dished up my cereal. Mother was reading a letter.

I tasted my cereal. It needed more sugar. "Take it easy," mother said. She didn't look up from the letter until she had turned the page that was half empty. Then she put her elbows on the table. She looked at me with her brown eyes. I knew something was up.

"Edey," she said, "that letter was from Uncle Paul."

I put my spoon into the cereal and stirred it around until the cream thinned it out like tan soup.

"Yeah?" I asked. "What's Captain Connell got to say?"

"Uncle Paul," mother corrected.

"He's not my uncle," I said.

Maybe I should tell about Paul. I've read lots of stories about mothers and their kids and wanting to get married again, the kids being jealous and all. I was never jealous of Paul. Honest truth. I just didn't like him. He's nice looking in a thin sort of way. He wears his uniform like he was one of the Three Musketeers. But his voice is as soft as a lady's. He likes people and nice places to eat and concerts and good books. I don't think he ever hauled off and socked anybody, even when he was a kid.

Before the war he was a professor somewhere. The second time he came to call on my mother—after seeing me, mind you—he brought me a doll. It looked exactly like the two blond girls down the street. Me, who hasn't played with dolls since I was two, if I did then, for which I was ashamed.

I'm not dumb. I know my mother's a young woman. She needs somebody to take care of her. But it made me sick the way she sort of got a jelly look on her face every time she looked at Paul Connell. If she had to fall for somebody, why couldn't it have been a real he-man like my father, who knew how to stake a tent and gaff a fish? Paul Connell would never shoot a gun, even to kill a bird, I bet. Which is why it was a good thing he was put in Washington as some sort of an adviser.

But I couldn't tell my mother all this. I couldn't tell her much of anything. I tried. Once I tried to show her how a model airplane was put together. You could see how mixed up it made her.

All she said to me was, "When I was your age I was learning to crochet." Crochet!

Before my father died, my mother went on a picnic with us, though. Only it was like taking one of the blond kids along. She squealed when she saw a snake. She was scared of the rowboat, a flat-bottomed old thing as safe as a cradle. Daddy took her home early. The next time she didn't go.

It was like that when he tried to teach her to play golf, too. She looked little and cute in her sweater and skirt and flat-heeled shoes. But she couldn't get the hitch of holding the club. After a while daddy said the words he used when he drove a ball into the rough. We went out alone from then on.

Mother was all right in the house, though. Daddy gave her that. She was a good cook. When daddy wasn't around, she played the piano for hours. He didn't care much for music. He didn't like to sit still.

I sure got away from mother and me at the breakfast table yesterday. Anyhow, she looked at me with those eyes that always seemed to ask something of me. It made me impatient.

"What's he want?" I said again. "I got to go fishing with Dud."

She folded part of the letter back and handed it to me. I read it.

"I'll be in Franklin Wednesday night, my dear," it said. "I can't believe it's coming true. Afterward, will you and your lovely daughter have dinner with me at the Lamont? She is lovely, Dora. I feel warm and tender toward her because she is yours. I hope this time I can somehow get her to be fond of me. We could have such a good life together, the three of us."

I didn't look right at mother. I knew she was waiting for me to say something. "Lovely." "Warm and tender." "Fond." I said it. "Slush," I said. "Slush."

Mother got up quickly. Not so fast that I couldn't see tears spring to her eyes. She pulled on her gloves. She put the letter into her purse.

"There's a surprise for you in my clothes closet,"

she said very quietly. "I wish you would do me the favor of wearing it tonight." She went out the door.

I slapped my spoon down on the table. Liza turned from the sink. Liza has been with us ever since mother got the job at the conservatory. She's apt to say what's on her mind. She did now.

"Trouble with you, Edey Hamilton," she said, "is you're jealous. Just plain nasty-mean jealous."

I didn't bend to answer her. I slammed the dining-room door hard and ran upstairs. "I'm not jealous," I said all the way up. "If it was any kind of a man but that sissy professor. That—that gentleman!"

I stood in my mother's room. I smelled lily of the valley. It choked in my throat. I was always hurting my mother. I didn't mean to. I didn't want to. But she was so darned awful gentle. Like Paul Connell. Like they didn't have any muscles in their hearts. Just mush and sweetness and light.

I got over feeling sorry when I looked at my surprise. It was pink, with two double ruffles on the bottom and little puffy sleeves. There was a white velvet jacket to go with it. I wouldn't wear that the longest day of my life!

Dud and I went to the yacht club to fish. The sun was out hot. It smelled like it held the day in its brightness. All the flowers and the lake and melted-tar taste of our lines. We went to our pier. It's rickety and away from the new dock. You can lie on your stomach and hold your pole out over the water and wait for the fish to bite.

Sometimes with Dud like that I almost felt daddy beside me. Of course, it was ridiculous. Daddy was six feet something and broad and firmed around the edges the way grown-ups are. Dud looks like something that isn't finished yet. He is going to be tall, because in the last year his head is way over mine. But his bones show on his face. His mouth looks loose and soft, like a girl's.

He's not like a girl, though, you can bet. Probably
Dud is the toughest boy going on sixteen in the
world. I don't mean bad tough like stealing cars or
that. I just mean that when we wrestle, which we
haven't done in a long time because he always makes
me cry quits, he feels strong. All knotty muscles and
good clean hard bones against me.

Dud and I have been friends since before daddy died.
There is a tree in his backyard and one in mine. We
used to climb up and be the general and his aide, each
in our own tree. What I liked about Dud was he was
always fair. I got to be the general every other day.

Playing with Dud, no matter what we did, I felt just
like a boy. I never felt that way with anybody else
except daddy. Mother, like I said, tried to make me
girlish. All her friends looked at me with a feather of
disgust tickling their noses. "She's such a roughneck
tomboy, Dora," they'd say. Funny, that made me
realize, surprised, that I was a girl.

Dud and I baited up our hooks. We lay for a long
time in the sun, not talking. My mind went hunting
for things and brought them back. Like a dog retriev-
ing old sticks and dried bones.

"What you thinking about?" Dud asked in the middle of it. "You had two nibbles and never noticed."

I pulled in my line. Sure enough, the bait was gone.
I fingered around in the rusty can for a fat worm. I
wanted to tell Dud what I was thinking. And I didn't
want to.

At last I said, "About going to the play last winter
with Paul Connell and my mother."

"What about it?"

I squashed the worm on the hook. It made a clear
circle before the water covered it. "He held my chair
for me. He brought us candy. He explained the
grown-up parts." I spit in the lake.

"Good shot," Dud said. He tilted his head and spit
farther. "What's wrong with that?" he asked.

"Sissy stuff," I said. There was a little pull on my line. I jerked the worm out of the water.

"Captain Connell is a good gent," Dud said.

"He's a sis," I insisted.

"Because he didn't get to shoot people in the war or because you're jealous of him?"

That hurt. Dud should know me better. "I'm not jealous!" I said. I yelled it out. "I'm not. I'm not!"

Dud looked at me carefully. He has very blue eyes with black lashes all around them. He scratched his nose. "Look, Edey," he said, "a boy in school felt like that. He didn't want anyone else to be with his mother. He spoiled it all. The man went away and his mother looks terrible."

I swallowed the lump in my throat. Dud always understood before. It was like the poetry. I didn't know how to say it. How to share it. I couldn't make the words come out. In my mind I was saying, *I want someone like daddy, Dud, or nobody at all. I don't care if my mother gets happy and spends most of her time with somebody else. Honest, I don't. Only, I'm lonely. If she married somebody like daddy, I could belong again.*

But all I could say was, "I couldn't stand that sissy underfoot all the time."

I never saw Dud's eyes like that before. For the first time I realized he was more than a year older than me. "Be your age, Edey," he said. "It's time you grew up. Connell's no more a sissy than—than you are."

It was a compliment, but I couldn't feel it. I was too taken up with the difference Dud had put between us. I pulled in my line and started back along the pier. I could hear his sneakers behind me. We walked up the yacht-club road. I didn't watch the shadows the trees on the bluff slapped across the path the way I usually did. Dud stayed a little behind me. When we got home, he cut through the bushes and I headed for my tree.

He stopped on his porch. "Don't be sore!" he called. "See you later!"

I climbed up the tree. I stayed there all afternoon. I was never so miserable in all my life.

Liza came out to hang up some clothes. She peered up at me. "Edey, you there?"

I didn't answer. Liza thought I was jealous. Mother thought I was jealous. Even Dud. Daddy would have understood. But he was dead.

Liza came closer. "I know you're there, Edey. And you come straight down. Your mother just called. She's bringing Captain Paul home before you all go out to dinner. She wants you should take a nice bath and put on your new dress."

She waited quite a while. Finally she shook her fist at me and went toward the house. She muttered, "That child. Selfish, spoiled—"

I put my hands over my ears. I heard the screen door slam just the same.

Pretty soon the sun cooled itself off to pale yellow. A taxi pulled up in front of the house. Captain Connell got out and reached in to help mother. He took her arm as if it was grandma's Spode cup. *Slush*, I thought. *Slush*.

I almost dozed. There was a crick in my right leg. I tried to straighten it. My left foot was asleep. The kitchen door slammed in Dud's house. He came out and got on his bicycle. He went fast down the street. He didn't even look toward the tree.

I knew my mother would come hunting me pretty soon. I tried to get it straight in my mind why I felt so bad. All I could do was to watch the way the sun hit underneath the leaves nearest me. It turned them veined and old. As though not only the tree had been alive for years, but the leaves knew it, too. What did they know? Everything, I decided. Everything that had happened in our backyard way before it was ours or anybody else's. Back when it was a tilled field. A wild forest with trees touching. The littlest leaf, born this summer, had some sort of a feeling that made it old and part of the tree.

That was the silly thing about my poetry thoughts. They didn't make sense. They just came out of me from something I didn't understand and couldn't put my finger on. Usually it was just the poetry. But now I couldn't put my finger on anything, it seemed like. Or my mother. Or Captain Connell. Or Dud. They all were away from me and something I couldn't understand.

Like you talk about the devil, and he comes out of the house. Captain Connell, I mean. He walked gently, like he talked. He put his feet down as easy as his words came out. He leaned against the tree and lit a cigarette. Everything got very still, the way it does sometimes in the late afternoon.

"Edey," he said slowly, "I wish we could be friends. It was tough enough making a wonderful woman like your mother love me. I don't see why she should."

Before I could stop myself I piped up, "I don't see why she should, either."

He didn't even lean his head back toward me. He shook it, instead. "You're right," he went on, as though it were sensible to carry on conversations with people up in trees you couldn't see. "I'm not good enough for her."

There was something about him that made me madder than ever. Daddy never would have talked like that. Daddy thought he was good enough for anybody. Everybody believed it, and he was.

Captain Connell flicked the ashes from his cigarette. "But she does love me. It's my good luck. Love is important, Edey. There's not nearly enough of it in the world."

"'Love,'" I said, again not meaning to. "Slush, you mean."

He stomped out the cigarette. I screamed inside of me, *go away. Go away.* I was afraid to say it.

"Who taught you to be so hard, Edey?" he asked at last. "It isn't right to be so hard."

I did scream then. "It isn't right to be so soft!" I cried. "Daddy told me to stand on my own feet! He said, 'Don't ask anything of anybody! Don't let yourself go mushy over people!' That's the trouble with you! And mother! You're mush! You're soft! I hate you!" I was crying something fierce when I stopped. I was scared. I expected the tree to fall down, and me in it.

Nothing happened, though. Except that Captain Connell walked very slowly and gently toward the house. He didn't even slam the door. I kept on crying. I remembered all the things daddy had told me. They didn't make me feel any better.

"People are weak," he'd said once when I was so tired from tennis I had to stop. "Never be weak, Edey. Push yourself physically. Then toughen your heart up. They'll sap your strength if you don't."

I didn't know what he meant then. I didn't really know now. All I knew was that I was ashamed and afraid of the way I'd talked to Captain Connell.

It began to fade out to twilight. After a while, Captain Connell and my mother came out of the house. They walked slowly down the street. He had his arm around her waist. My mother didn't seem to bounce the way she usually does. Her back looked tired.

Liza shut the door and shuffled across the alley on her way to her sister's. I climbed down from the tree. I felt stiff all over. Dud's bicycle was still gone. I walked down the alley to the back road and started toward the yacht club. I'd never been there so late in the day. The tree shadows were black fingers now. They stretched and curled. I was scared. I couldn't stop going ahead. I couldn't hurry. It was full dark when I started out on the old pier. I got to the end of it before I saw that somebody was there before me. It was too late to turn back.

It was Dud. "Hi," he said. "No bites."

His fish pole made a dim, slim lightness against the black water. His back was propped up against his bicycle wheel.

"You didn't come home for supper," I said.

"Nope. Brought a sandwich. Two of them. I've got half left."

He pushed it toward me. I bit into it without thinking. It was cheese and peanut butter. It made my mouth turn wet. I thought back to my breakfast. It seemed a long time ago. A star exploded without any noise. I could feel Dud beside me like warm waves. He moved his pole up and down. You could almost see it in the star shine. Almost, but not quite.

Something hurt inside of me. I couldn't stand it. I felt Dud, but I wasn't close to him. I'd never be close to him again. The lump in my throat exploded like the star. I started to cry. In all the years, Dud had never seen me cry. Not even when I got my finger stove in a baseball game. He couldn't see me now, but he could hear me. The sobs wouldn't stay swallowed.

"Hey," he said. "Edey." He was quiet for a minute. "Edey," he said again. His voice was different. I felt his hand on my arm, like we were wrestling. I tried to pull away, but I knew he was stronger. He yanked me up against him. "Don't cry," he said softly. His breath touched my cheek. "Edey, don't cry."

"I'm not—" I started.

He stopped me. He stopped me with his mouth against my lips. His mouth wasn't soft the way I thought. It was hard, like his hands, like his chest. He held it there for a long time. Then he let me go. I slapped him, hard. I felt the bones of his cheek under my fingers. I got up and ran for home as fast as I could.

Everything in me was crying when I got up to my room. I sat down in the window seat without turning on the lights. I cried and cried. Dud, too. He was soft and slushy. Everything was kissing and loving and foolishness. Dud had done something terrible. He had put a difference between us. Things would never be the same again. I'd never feel like a boy, all strong and hard and outdoorsy again.

I turned on the light after a while. I looked at myself in the mirror. My face seemed fatter. My eyes were red, but my lips were redder. I went in the bathroom and started to run a cold shower the way daddy taught me. But instead I plugged the bathtub, ran warm water and put a handful of my mother's bath salts in it. I sat a long time in the steam and warmness.

Back in my room, I looked at myself again. My hair curled a little like mother's. I held it up away from my neck and reached for a barrette to pin it. Then I went into mother's room and brought the pink dress back. I put it on. It felt slippery against my skin. It fitted tight around my waist. The skirt swirled out. I made circles, watching the skirt stand stiff around my ankles.

I didn't know my mother was back until I heard her call me. "Edey," she said, "come down, dear. We're going to have some scrambled eggs and toast."

I didn't answer. I felt guilty. Like the time she caught me shuffling the candy around in her Easter box so the gaps where I'd eaten out wouldn't show.

I sat in the window seat and spread the slippery pink skirt out around me. Dud would come and beg my forgiveness on bended knee. "Think nothing of it, pal," I'd say. I'd give him a hearty slap on the back. "Let's forget this foolishness and play catch."

Or I would put my hand gently on his bleached hair. "Dud," I'd say, "it was stronger than you. Stronger than I—" I remembered the play Captain Connell took us to, where the leading lady said that.

What was stronger, I asked myself. *What?* I began to get a wonderful glowing thought. Something was stronger than Dud's being strong or my being strong.

With muscles, I mean. Something made Dud kiss me when he probably most likely didn't want to at all. Captain Connell's words came clear to me, "Love is important, Edey."

The smell of coffee moved up the stairs. It crawled into my nose. It was bigger than the thing I had almost found out. I was so hungry all of a sudden that my stomach ached with it. I got up. I ran down the steps as fast as I could. I smelled toast burning. I pushed open the kitchen door. I blinked in the light. When my eyes unfuzzed, I saw my mother pulling herself out from the circle of Captain Connell's arms. Her cheeks were red. Her lips were shiny. Her eyes looked startled and pleading.

A picture came to me. I remembered the kitchen like this. My mother stood in front of daddy. Her hands were on his arms. Her eyes looked the same as they did now. "David," she'd said. Her voice was like an old bell that has run the same tune until it's rusted tired. "David, please be kind to me. Just once in a while. Please be—"

I didn't remember the rest she'd said. Daddy turned, saw me, pushed mother's arms away and told me about a new rod.

Now her eyes were the same. Her voice, too, when she spoke to me. "Edey," she said, "Edey I wanted to come right up and tell you. But Paul said—" She stopped. Her eyes widened until they filled her face. "Edey, darling!" she cried. "You've got the new dress on!"

I looked at it. I rubbed my hand against the cool, slippery skirt. I had forgotten.

"Tell me what?" I asked.

Captain Connell put his arm around my mother. She leaned back against him. I could tell she didn't even know it. "That we were married this afternoon, Edey," he said in his quiet way. "We wanted you to come, but you seemed—" he smiled a little with one corner of his mouth "—to prefer being alone."

It was as if somebody had hit me in the stomach. I could feel how mad I was way deep inside. But I wasn't mad at them, I realized all at once. I was mad at me. I shut myself out. Sitting up in a tree like a long-legged bird. Feeling sorry for myself. When I could have been seeing my mother married. I could have been part of them, close, the way they were close now. I could have helped to make her happy.

Instead of which, they probably hated me. Dud hated me for slapping him. I hated myself. It was terrible. I started to choke and I started to cry. I scrubbed the tears out with my fists. Three times in one day. Me, who never cried.

My mother's arms came around me. Soft and sweet and somehow like they held out the whole world. "Darling," she whispered. "Edey, baby, don't cry." Like Dud. "Don't cry. We didn't mean to hurt you."

I pulled away from her, but I held on to her hand so she'd know I wasn't "just like my father."

"I'm not hurt," I said. My voice sounded little. I reached my eyes to Captain Connell's. "I'm not hurt. I'm just sorry." I choked and blubbered. "Mother," I cried, "I'm sorry!"

She was crying, too. "Edey," she said. She lifted her head from my hair. "Paul, see? I told you. Paul, she is a little like me!"

He came over and put his arms around us both. They were hard, with long slim muscles. "Of course she is," he said. "And there's no better way to be."

I don't know who laughed first, but somebody did. I felt better. I began to feel grand. The feeling swelled inside of me and filled everything but my stomach. "I'm starved," I said. "Let's eat."

Mother put more eggs in the pan; I watched the toast. Uncle Paul poured some milk into glasses. Suddenly I heard Dud's whistle outside. I stood stockstill. My heart pounded like the eighth inning of a tough baseball game. I didn't move.

"Isn't that Dud?" mother asked. "Darling, invite him in. We'll have a celebration."

I moved toward the back door like I was in a dream. I was scared to step out of the bright kitchen. I took a long time to go down the dark path toward the tree.

Dud stepped out and came toward me. "Mrs. Hamilton," he said. He sounded like he'd been running. "Is Edey home? I didn't mean to—" He stopped.

"It's not 'Mrs.' Hamilton," I said. This time I sounded like myself. A small leftover laugh tickled against my throat. "It's 'Miss' Hamilton, to you."

The moon came out suddenly. He leaned toward me. His eyes were dark and pointed. "Edey," he whispered. "Edey!"

The laugh jumped out. I whirled around. "What you think, pal?" I asked. "Can I play on your team?"

He laughed, too. A very happy sound. "Anytime, kid," he said. He touched my dress with one finger. His voice changed. "I came over to say I'm sorry, Edey," he said slowly.

My heart pounded again. I knew, but something made me ask, "Sorry for what?"

He swallowed hard. The swallow carried over into his words. "For—for kissing you. I shouldn't have done that."

I made myself sound cross. "You certainly shouldn't have," I said. He looked at me quickly. "But, then," I went on, "I shouldn't have slapped you." I put out my hand. "If you'll forget it, I will."

His hand felt big around mine. I never felt so little before. "I can't forget it—the kiss, I mean. But I promise not to do it again." He squeezed my hand. "That is, until you grow up."

Suddenly that was the funniest thing of all. I laughed, and he did, too. I pulled him toward the house. I could see how it would be in the kitchen. The four of us around the table. A dozen eggs apiece to eat, if we wanted. I felt like I'd just found out how good it was to eat. I felt like I could never get enough of the eggs, the kitchen. Or mother or Uncle Paul... or Dud. I started to run. I couldn't wait for us all to be together.

"Hold up that skirt!" Dud called as he passed me. "You're a big girl now!"

I pulled the ruffles to my knees. I put an extra spurt of speed into my swing. I gained on Dud. I caught up with him. We were together when we ran through the kitchen door.

"Tomboy," mother said when I skidded to a stop beside her. But she didn't sigh. She smiled. Her eyes looked at me as though we two had a secret. She kissed me quickly. I kissed her back. She whispered in my ear, "Oh, Edey, I'm so happy."

I looked at her. "I'm happy, too," I said. I really was. *Maybe it's not so bad to be a woman,* I thought. *Maybe it's not bad at all.*

The moonlight walked in my window and settled itself comfortably on the foot of my bed. The day was far behind me. Fishing. The tree. The littlest leaf. Uncle Paul. The way Dud watched me in the pink dress.

I closed my eyes. I thought of daddy. His face kept getting mixed up with Uncle Paul's. With mother's happy look. With Dud. *"Toughen your heart up,"* daddy had said. *"They'll sap your strength."*

I put my hand on my chest. My ribs were hard, like nailed-down steel. But under them I could feel my heart. It beat with a softness. With a sweet easy softness. It wasn't tough at all. Yet I never felt so strong in my life.

I woke up out of the black-velvet place in the morning. I pulled up the curtain and looked out the window. Dud's curtain was up, too, although it was very early. "Something wonderful will happen today." The words sang themselves until they filled all of me.

It was different from any other morning. Today something wonderful really would happen.

I ran over to my desk. I pulled out my five-year diary. The poetry slid from my mind down to my fingers and off the tip of my pencil: "The littlest leaf knows all the things the trees holds in its heart."

You're invited to accept 4 books and a surprise gift Free!

Acceptance Card

Mail to: **Harlequin Reader Service**®

In the U.S.
2504 West Southern Ave.
Tempe, AZ 85282

In Canada
P.O. Box 2800, Postal Station A
5170 Yonge Street
Willowdale, Ontario M2N 6J3

YES! Please send me 4 free Harlequin Romance® novels and my free surprise gift. Then send me 6 brand new novels every month as they come off the presses. Bill me at the low price of $1.65 each ($1.75 in Canada)—an 11% saving off the retail price. There are no shipping, handling or other hidden costs. There is no minimum number of books I must purchase. I can always return a shipment and cancel at any time. Even if I never buy another book from Harlequin, the 4 free novels and the surprise gift are mine to keep forever.

116 BPR-BPGE

Name _____ (PLEASE PRINT)

Address _____ Apt. No. _____

City _____ State/Prov. _____ Zip/Postal Code _____

This offer is limited to one order per household and not valid to present subscribers. Price is subject to change.

ACR-SUB-1